Grandma's Silent Auction
November
BY: Michael James

Copyright © 2020 by Michael James

All rights reserved.

No part of this book may be reproduced in any form or by any electronic or mechanical means, including information storage and retrieval systems, without written permission from the author, except for the use of brief quotations in a book review.

CHAPTER ONE
CIARA

Last night I officially broke up with Adler. I crawled into my bed with my best friend next to me with a sad heart and cried myself to sleep. I had a crazy dream and when I woke up this morning, I knew what I needed to do next. If I am going to begin to build a wonderful life with a man, there's something I know I must do first. I know in my heart, this dream is right. I haven't been this sure until now.

I roll over and shake Porter awake. He peeks at me with only one eye open.

"I need your help."

"This early in the morning?"

"It's not all that early. You are actually late for opening my store."

"Fuck!"

"Chill it's no big deal. Let's go get one of Katie's famous muffins."

"Now you're talking."

"We can talk about the help I need over breakfast."

"Wait, how are you this cheerful this morning."

"I got some clarity in my sleep!"

I jump out of bed. *"Let's go! Get your booty out of bed."*

"Gee whiz, I'm coming."

I practically skip out of the room. I feel weird, that's a given, but it's a good weird. I laugh when I look past my shoulder and see Porter rubbing his eyes as he follows me down the hall. I love my best friend. He puts up with all of my moods and never complains. He literally is the only person who has never walked out of my life. Well, besides Grams. I know that I can always depend on him. We will forever be best friends.

I put the water on for tea and then get Porter and myself muffins. I take the plates over and set them down. I glance at him. Poor guy. He looks exhausted.

"Why are you so tired today? Did I keep you awake?"

"No. I was up for a long time."

"What do you mean?"

"After I got Cora's outfits all ready to ship, I went

out. I met someone. Let's just say, I never made it to bed until last night."

"Oh you naughty boy! Do tell me the details."

"I went to an after party with this girl. When the party died down we left together."

"Did you do it?"

"Nope! I took her to her place, she cooked me breakfast and then we stayed up talking."

"What's her name?"

"Robin."

"Are you going to see her again?"

"I got her number, so it's possible."

I smile. Yay for Porter. He needs a real lady in his life instead of all the one-night stands he has.

I got to the stove and poured two cups of hot water. I grab both cups in one hand, then get the container of teabags. I set it all down. We both start picking through it for what flavor we want.

"Okay, baby girl, spill. What do you need my help with?"

"I want to go to Paris."

"What? When?"

"As soon as possible."

"Why this sudden urge to go to Paris?"

"I want time to think about what I'm going to do. I don't think I can do that here."

"How long are you going for?"

"Well, I'm not sure yet! I do have two weeks left in this month that I was supposed to be with Adler."

"I've got to admit, I'm jealous. What do you need my help with?"

"I don't want anyone to know where I'm at, especially Grams. I have no idea where I should stay or even what to visit while I'm there."

"I'll be glad to help you. If your grandmother asks me where you are, I'm not sure I can keep that a secret."

"Fair enough. Just don't let it slip out before I get there."

🐞

It's been a very long day. It's one in the morning and I am sitting in a seat on a plane that's ready to take off any second to Paris. I am so excited. I cannot believe I'm finally going to a place I've always wanted to go. As much as I am excited, it doesn't seem to help my anxiety any. My stomach is still knotted knowing we are about to take off. I have a purpose for this trip. This plane ride is going to be just fine. I'm going to be perfectly fine. Nothing is going to happen to me. This plane isn't going to

CHAPTER 1

crash. I put my earbuds in and close my eyes. I need my mind to relax. I think about the pictures I saw of the hotel l will be staying in. I try to imagine what the places I want to see look like in person. I tell myself this plane ride is worth every second of misery in the end. All I have to do is make it through this seven hour flight.

I open my eyes to find the lights have been dimmed. I look around and see that I'm the only one who still has their seatbelt on. So I unbuckle my belt and get out of my seat to stretch my legs. How long have I been asleep? I rub my arms as I walk toward the restroom. It's a little chilly on the flight. I scan the aisle as I walk quietly. Almost everyone is taking a nap. I can't blame them since we left at one in the morning.

I use the bathroom and when I come out, there's a man standing close by. He's a bit older than I am. Quite handsome for a man his age. Porter would call him a silver fox if he saw him.

"Is it your first trip to Paris?"
"It is. How about you?"
"You are going to love it."
"I'm looking forward to it."
"I hope you have a pleasant time."
"Thank you."

He nods his head, then enters the restroom. I make my way back to my seat. I should probably try to get some more sleep. I wish I had a blanket, though.

I feel a tap on my shoulder. I look up to see the silver fox towering above me. Not who I was hoping to see. I smile because I don't know what else to do.

"Care to join me in a nightcap?"

"Nightcap, huh?"

"Okay, an early morning breakfast of champs."

"I think I'm going to try and get some more shut-eye."

"If you change your mind, I'm in first class."

"Thank you."

I lean into the aisle and see him walking into first class. Then I look around and catch an older lady giving me the evil eyes. Chill lady, I don't want the hot older man. I see her pulling the night mask down on her eyes. I guess we might have woken her up.

"I think I will have that drink," I say loud enough for her to hear, but not overly too loud to wake the entire plane.

I enter first class and I see a small glow of light. I go to it. *"I changed my mind."*

"Lovely, please have a seat."

"I'm Ciara."

"I'm Jacob."

CHAPTER 1

The stewardess came over to us. Jacob asks what I would like. *"I'll just have a glass of orange juice."*

"Breakfast drinks it is!"

He tells the stewardess two glasses of orange juice with champagne. He winks at me. *"A drink is not a drink without champagne."*

I let out a little laugh. *"Why are you going to Paris?"*

"I'm going home. I travel to the States often for my job."

It doesn't take the stewardess long to bring our drinks. Jacob must have picked up that I'm cold because he asks for a blanket. When she brings it, I wrap it around me.

"Are you married, Jacob?"

"I am. Been close to twenty years. I don't see a ring on your finger."

"I might be getting engaged soon. What advice would you give a girl about to be married?"

We continue to talk for a few hours. I eventually fell asleep listening to him talking. He has a very calming voice.

CHAPTER TWO
CIARA

Yesterday I checked into the hotel. I am so thrilled to be here. My room is magnificent in so many ways. It is way above any place I have ever stayed before when it comes to luxury. Not that I have done much vacationing in the past to compare it to, but I have traveled for fashion shows before. Porter did a wonderful job helping me book this room.

The first thing I did after getting settled into my room, I got ready to go and find some breakfast. Leaving the hotel I was quickly reminded about the time difference. I found a sweet spot to fill my stomach. After dinner I walked around and did a little window shopping. Lord knows I don't need any more clothing. Before I leave, I will be getting something nice for Porter. He would just about die if he had something in his wardrobe from Paris. I might have to get him a few things so that he isn't constantly wearing the same thing.

After I walked the streets for what seemed like hours, I got a little lost. I had to flag down a cab to get me back to the hotel. Come to find out, I wasn't even that far away. Hopefully I won't be getting lost too often.

I wasn't overly tired, but I figured I should get to bed at a decent hour if I wanted to get on Paris time. I woke up this morning ready to start my day. I did my normal routine of showering and dressing for the weather. When I was ready, I left the hotel to find a place to eat. This time, I didn't go quite so far. I stopped at the first cafe I found. I'm already learning new things. In America they say breakfast should be the biggest meal of the day. Here they have a croissant or toast with honey or jam. Lunch is the biggest meal of the day. I don't need a big breakfast. If I'm at Grams' I only have a muffin. Before moving back with her, I didn't really eat at all. Maybe I'm French!

I pay my bill. I sat here longer than I intended. Today is one of those days that I have something I need to do. I'm quite a bit nervous about it. I sat here trying to build the courage to do what I'm about to do.

I flag down a cab and give the driver an address.

He raised his brow at me. When he moved into traffic and only went a few blocks, I felt foolish. I could have walked.

Getting out of the car, I look at the sign on the side of the building. *"Kirkwood studio of Design,"* I say to no one but myself. I take a few steps toward the entrance. My nerves are rattling inside me. I tell myself I've come this far and I can't turn back now. So I take the last few steps and pull the door open. I breathe in the air that is circling around in the air. It smells like sandalwood. I am greeted right away.

"Can I help you find anything?"

"I'm wondering if I can see the owner."

"I'm sorry, the owner doesn't come in on Sundays."

"I see. I'll come back another day. Thank you for your help."

I practically ran out of there to flag down another cab. When I get into the backseat, I dig in my purse for the piece of paper I wrote on this morning. I hand it to the driver, hoping I'm not made to look like a foolish American again. The driver whips out into traffic. I grab the car's handle as he weaves through traffic. My nerves are already on edge and if he keeps driving like this I may have a break down before I get there.

CHAPTER 2

I look at my watch. It's only a little after nine. Maybe I should have the driver turn around and I come back later in the day. It is a Sunday after all. I might not have thought this through enough.

"We're here. That will be fifteen euros."

Shit! I glance out the window. It's not too late, I can still go back to the hotel. Go about my day doing something else.

The driver twists in his seat and holds out his hand. Shit, shit, shit! What do I do? I look out the window again. Fuck it! I came all this way, I shouldn't turn back now.

I get out the money and pay him. *"Can you wait in case I won't be staying?"*

"I'll wait one minute."

"Thank you."

I get out and straighten my jacket. My hands are sweaty. My heart is thumping in my chest. I walk to the front entrance and knock. I look at the cab driver and he takes off. Asshole! I knock again and the front door opens.

"Hello."

"Hi," I say, *"I'm not sure I'm in the right place or not. Is this the home of Mr. Kirkwood?"*

"You have come to the right place."

"Is he home?"

"Yes, my dear, he is. Come on in."

I look over my shoulder. It's not too late to run. I close my eyes briefly before I step into the house. The woman smiles a warm welcoming smile.

"I hope I'm not interrupting anything."

"Not at all." She leads me to a room with very large French doors. I follow her in. *"Please make yourself comfortable. I'll be right back."*

My eyes scan the family room. This room is very elegant. Fresh flowers in vases throughout the room. A fireplace in the middle far wall. It's not lit, but I bet it gives off a relaxing feel when it is. I sit on the sofa and cross my legs, keeping my back straight. I glance toward the entryway and gasp when he enters. He comes right to me and holds out his hand.

"Ms. Verbank, welcome to my home."

"You know who I am?"

"I know your face and the name that goes along with it. Other than that, I do not know you. This is my wife, Molena."

"Hello, it's nice to meet you."

They both sit down and we all just look at each other. The silence is deafening. They seem nice, but I probably shouldn't have come here.

I clear my voice. *"How do you know my face and my name?"*

CHAPTER 2

"Darling, you're in all the tabloids," Molena says.

Not the answer I was hoping for. *"I see. I thought... I hope they aren't as cruel here as they are in America."* I do a nervous laugh.

"We don't believe most of what was printed."

"Good, I guess." I take a deep breath. *"Mr. Kirkwood..."*

"Let me stop you right there," his voice is soft when he speaks. *"Please, call me Ciaro."*

"Okay."

"Ciara, I believe... we believe we know why you are here."

"You do?"

"You think I'm your father."

I feel like I'm going to get sick. *"I don't know for sure."*

"I don't know either. Molena here saw your face in the tabloids last month and said you look a hell of a lot like me. I thought my wife was crazy until I saw your last name."

"So you do know Cassidy Verbank?"

"I did briefly many years ago, yes."

"I'm almost twenty-six. My birthday is next month."

"That is the right timing."

"I only recently learned your name. My mother left me before I turned five. I spoke to her for the first time since she left and she told me your name."

"Oh, dear," Molena says.

"I didn't know about you."

"I know, she told me that too."

"What do you want from me?"

"Nothing. I just wanted a chance to meet you."

"Molena and I would like it very much if you would stay for lunch. I would love to get to know you a little."

I am a bit surprised by the invitation. Honestly, I thought they would think I was crazy, then send me on my merry way. I was not expecting them to be so kind to me.

"I don't want to intrude. I just showed up here unannounced and kind of dropped this news on your laps."

"Ciaro and I were going to wait until after the holidays to take a trip to New York."

"You are going to New York?"

"Yes, sweetie, to find you. Ciaro and I couldn't stop wondering if you're his daughter."

"Oh." I feel my face getting hot. Is it hot in here? Is this really happening? My father wants to know

me? *"Don't you want proof before you get to know me?"*

"Let me show you something."

Ciaro stands and walks over to a bookshelf and gets a green album. He brings it over to where I am sitting.

"May I," he asks with his hand motioning at the spot next to me.

"Of course."

He opens the album and shows me a picture. *"That was my mother. I think that is all the proof I need."*

Tears fill my eyes. I look just like her. Molena says she's going to give us time to ourselves. I am spending time with my father. It's a bit overwhelming, but in a very good way.

CHAPTER THREE
CIARA

I feel like I am a brand new person. I no longer have to wonder who my father is. Ciaro and Molena welcomed me into their home and lives yesterday without hesitation. I couldn't be more pleased to know my father is a very kind man. We can never make up for lost time, but we have the future. I had no idea until yesterday how much I missed out on. Most of my life I only cared why my mother left me. It didn't leave much room to wonder who he was. My mother not only robbed me from knowing Ciaro, but she robbed him too. We were both cheated out of having a relationship because Cassidy is a selfish human being. I am no longer going to worry about the woman who gave birth to me. I want her out of my thoughts. No more is she going to keep Ciaro away from me. Yesterday I got his side of the story. I whole heartedly believe him because he doesn't have reason to lie. His side of the story seems more realistic than Cassidy's. The way he put it, they met at a mutual friends party. They liked each other right off the bat. Or at least that's what he thought. After a few weeks of being with each other every day, he caught her with another man. He was upset and decided he wasn't going to stick around. He had dreams to fulfill so he bought a ticket to Paris and never looked back. I am super excited to see his dream today. Ciaro is picking me up soon and taking me to Kirkwood Studio of Design. I guess cloth designing didn't just come from Grams.

Walking into Kirkwood Studio of Design next to Ciaro is going to be nerve racking. Without knowing how he'll introduce me to people is making me anxious. Will I be Ciara Verbank or will I be his daughter? The question keeps running through my mind over and over. It's to the point of making me feel nauseous. I tell myself everything is going to be fine, that it doesn't matter how he introduces me. We know who I am to him and that's all that should matter. I just wish these nerves would stop.

Of course I had myself all worked up for nothing. Everything went fine going with Ciaro to his business. He introduced me as his daughter, Ciara. He took the time to show me around his store and work area. His designs are amazing. Honestly, I am in awe of this man. He is so kind, easy to talk to, and is one hell of a designer. I saw awards lining the walls in his office. He told me he stopped doing shows about fifteen years ago. I would have been round ten. Now I know why I haven't recognized his name. If I saw his stuff in a fashion show, I'd never forget his name.

After Ciaro showed me everything, he asked if I wanted to join him for lunch. I happily agreed. My time with him is limited. My main purpose to come here was to meet him, but I also came here to think. I have difficult choices to make ahead of me and I really need to sort out who I see myself with.

I am quite surprised that we came to Ciaro's home for lunch. I thought we would hit up a restaurant or deli. Molena has the table set for three and ready when we get here. I learned that they believe lunch should be the biggest meal of the day, but I wasn't expecting it to be what we Americans would have for

CHAPTER 3

dinner. A glass of wine with lunch is perfectly okay with me.

"So, Ciara, how was your visit to Ciaro's pride and joy?"

"It was wonderful! I am highly impressed with his work."

"I've been looking at your work, you are remarkable yourself, Ciara."

My smile grows large. A compliment from my father is heartwarming. Tears build in my eyes. He reaches over and puts a hand on my shoulder.

"I'm okay," I say.

"You are okay. I can see you turned out to be a lovely young woman. I'll have to thank your grandmother for doing a wonderful job of raising my daughter. I wish I could have done that myself."

I excuse myself to use the restroom. I need a moment alone to get my thoughts together. I break. The tears come on stronger. My father wishes he raised me! My heart is overflowing with happiness. I don't see how meeting Ciaro would be possible, if it weren't for Wyatt. I don't know how I'm ever going to be able to thank him.

After getting myself put back together, I join Ciaro and Molena back at the table. I can see it in their eyes, they want to ask if I'm alright. I hope they don't. I'll break all over again.

"How did you two meet?"

They look at each other. These two people have true love. It is written all over their faces. Molena is the first to speak.

"We met on a tour here in Paris. Ciaro was only here for a week or so. I was with a friend just out for the day." They take each other's hand. *"I saw him just a few people ahead of me and was attracted right away. He turned around, our eyes connected and I was instantly blushing. We didn't talk that day. About a month later I was leaving a coffee shop and he was coming in at the same time. I walked right into him. When I looked up at him, I knew he was the same man from the tour. My cheeks warmed the second he spoke to me. He asked me if I wanted to join him for tea. I wouldn't have turned him down for all the money in the world. The rest is history. I found the love of my life."*

"That's so sweet. By tea do you mean just tea, or was it dinner?"

"Dinner. I took Molena to a quiet place not too far from here. We talked for hours and hours. I knew at that point coming to Paris was the greatest choice I ever made." My lips barely curl when I smile.

"Ciara, I have thought about this since I learned you might've been my daughter. If I did know about you, I wouldn't have left the States. I wouldn't have been with your mother, but I would have been a father to you."

"I believe you."

"I'm sorry I wasn't there for you."

"You are here now, right?"

"I am and I'm not going anywhere."

"Neither am I," Molena adds.

"I do want to know something. It's really been on my mind a lot."

"Okay."

"What's the deal with all gossip in the tabloids?"

"You mean all the men and why are they calling me nasty names?"

"Yes."

I start from the beginning and tell Ciaro and Molena all about Grams' auction she has every year, the charity and what it means to her. Then I tell them about her auctioning me off to ten men and how I've dated one a month for the past ten months. Surprised isn't a word I would use to explain his expression. I think he was a bit angry. I told them I was angry at the whole situation at first, until I met Malcolm.

"He's the one you love?"

"I do love him. The problem is, I love more than one man. I'm really confused about who I love the most."

"You want to marry one of these men?"

"I don't know that either. I mean, I want marriage. I just don't know if it will be a December wedding."

"Marriage isn't a game."

"I know."

"What Molena and I didn't tell you about our love story is that we married three weeks after our first date. I knew when I asked her to be my wife, I knew without a doubt she was the one for me."

"What made you so sure?"

"Your soul has a way of speaking to you if you listen to what it has to say. I couldn't imagine a day going by without having Molena beside me. She lit a fire inside me that my soul craved. If one of those men speaks to you like that, you'll have love."

"How will I know if he feels that way about me? I'm scared I'll choose one man, and learn I am not what he wants."

"Sweetheart, trust me, you will know all on you our own if you just listen and the rest will be easy to figure out."

I don't fully understand what he means, but I'll pretend that I do. *"Thank you for the advice."*

"Whenever you need someone to talk to, I'm here for you now."

"Thank you." I give him a big smile. *"Why are you two not parents?"*

They both look at each other and back to me. Molena says, *"We are parents. We didn't want to overwhelm you all at once. Your father and I have a daughter."*

"Oh. Where is she? Will I be meeting her?"

"Her name is Celine. She's away at college studying to be a doctor. We plan on telling her about you when she comes home for the holidays."

"I will be gone by then."

"Molena and I both feel it's important for the two of you to meet. So, we would like to bring Celine to meet you after the new year."

"I'd like that. Thank you."

We long ago finished eating. When Ciaro looked at his watch, I thought for sure he was going to take me back to my hotel. He didn't though, he said it was still early enough to catch the tour if I want to go. The same one where he and Molena first saw each other. I wasn't turning down that invitation.

CHAPTER FOUR
CIARA

I have been in Paris for a week now and I have spent every day with my father and his wife. I booked a flight for home last night when I got back to my room. I packed and was ready to leave once I left the hotel this morning. I have been enjoying every second I have spent with them, however, I'm not spending as much time thinking about what I'm going to do. Next week Grams expects me to be deciding who I want to be with and start the process of officially breaking up with nine men. To my knowledge she doesn't know I'm not with Adler. The night that I left Adler's and went home, she wasn't there. I was gone before she even got back. As much as I want to stay and get to know my father more, I know I have men back in the States waiting for my answer. I can't decide here when I'm spending all my time with

Ciaro. This afternoon I said my goodbyes and told him and Molena I'll see them after the New Year. I can't put into words how wonderful it felt for him to hug me. It truly hurt having to say goodbye. Ciaro wanted to bring me to the airport, but I told him it was easier for me to go alone. He didn't like it, but respected my wishes.

I give my ticket to the flight attendant and she tells me I've been upgraded to first class. I told her there must be a mistake. She assured me it wasn't. I scan the airport and I see him. I wave and my father nods his head. I want to run to him and wrap my arms around him. I don't have time to do that. My plane is boarding.

I found my seat and set the blank journal Adler gave me on the seat next to me. I settle in, getting my seatbelt secured. Before I begin to write, I put my earbuds in and selected my favorite playlist. I'm going to use this flight home to figure out where my heart belongs. I want a forever relationship like Ciaro and Molena have. Grams was never in a serious relationship for me to see what love looks like firsthand. I don't really have that many friends to witness it that way, either. I saw it this past week and I want it more than ever.

I put the pen to the paper. Where do I start? How do I figure out who my soulmate is? I think about how Ciaro said to listen to my inner self and I'll know. I close the book and put it off to the side. I thought I could figure everything out on paper, but I think I'm wrong. I'm just going to have to face each man and really listen to what my soul says to me.

The flight home went off without problems. Since it was so late, I took a taxi home. I went back to my apartment, I should say. When I entered, I remembered Grams had all my stuff moved to the mansion. I stuck around my old place for a while thinking. Locking up my apartment, I thought about possibly renting my apartment out. It seems I won't be needing it, since home is now the mansion again.

In the time I spent thinking, I figured out the first person I need to see. I left my old place with a heavy heart. The next few weeks are going to be tough. Breaking up with such wonderful men is going to be downright heartbreaking. I know it needs to be done, though.

I was able to sneak in without waking Grams. I

still have no idea if she knows I went to Paris or not, but I plan on telling her in the morning. I am actually really excited to tell her I met my father. Right now, I need to get some rest. I slept some on the plane. Not enough, though. I'm pretty damn tired.

CHAPTER FIVE
CIARA

I walk into the kitchen and see Grams having her tea and muffin while doing something on her phone. Whatever it is she's doing it has her attention as she hasn't even noticed my presence. Katie on the other hand does, so she gets me a muffin and I take it to the breakfast table.

"Good morning, Grams."

She looks up from her phone. "Good morning, dear."

Why is she not all that surprised to see me? "How are you doing?"

"I'm doing wonderful. How about you?"

"I am doing okay."

I take a bite of my muffin and Katie brings hot water over for me. She also refills Grams' cup. We both stare at each other briefly before I make my tea.

CHAPTER 5

"Are you going to spill the beans about what happened with you and Adler?"

"We just aren't meant to be together, I guess. The first week we were together was great. Then we just fell apart."

"How was your week in Paris?"

"So you know about that?"

"Adler came to see me. He wanted to give me a check."

"Check for what?"

"Bigger donation for my charity. Hundred thousand more on top of his bid to date you."

"That's really sweet."

"I guess you made quite the impression on him."

"That doesn't explain how you knew I went to Paris."

"When Adler came here he told me you two broke up two days before he came to see me. I was worried about you, so I asked a little bird to find out where you went off to."

"Did you have Wyatt track my phone again?"

"No, I asked Porter."

I eat some of my muffin and drink my tea. Grams sips her tea while her eyes remain on me. I can't hold back anymore.

"Have you ever heard the name Ciaro Kirkwood before?"

"The famous clothing designer?"

"That's the one."

"His work is award winning from what I remember."

"Have you ever met him?"

"Not that I can recall. Why did you meet him in Paris?"

"I did."

"That must have been nice."

"Grams, I didn't tell you something about when I saw Cassidy." She sets her tea cup down. "She told me Ciaro is my father."

"So you went off to find out? Ciara, you know how your mother lies..."

I interrupt her. *"He is my father."*

Grams pushes her chair out from under the table. Stands and takes her cup to the sink. She stands over the sink without saying a word. She then stands tall and rubs her temples before turning to face me.

"Did he know about you all these years?"

"No. He knew nothing about me. He said if he had, he would have raised me."

"How can you be so sure he's your father?"

"I look a lot like him. He showed me a picture of

CHAPTER 5

his mother and I could be her twin. He said he was with Cassidy about that time, as well. He left the states after he caught her cheating. So it would have been before she knew she was pregnant."

"Does he want a relationship with you?"

"Yes. He is a very kind man. I met his wife, Molena, as well. They have a daughter that I haven't met yet, but they plan on bringing her here to meet me after all the holidays."

"I'm happy for you."

"Ciaro is looking forward to getting to know you. He wants to thank you for raising me."

"I don't need anyone to thank me for that. I'd do it a hundred times over if I had to."

"Are you upset? You seem upset."

"No, Ciara, I'm not upset that you found your father."

"But you are upset about something

"Not at all. I am proud of you, sweetheart. I wanted you to spread your wings and see everything life has to offer. I see that you have done that. That takes courage. This year you've grown so much. I couldn't be any more proud of you than I am right now."

I get up and hug my grandma. I love this woman so very much. She is my world and has been my entire life. If it weren't for her, I'd be stuck in a bad relationship and I probably never would have found my father.

"I love you, Grams."

"I love you, dear." She kisses my cheek. *"Now tell me more about Ciaro."*

We sit back at the table, have more tea as I tell her all about my dad and Molena. I literally cannot stop smiling. Grams is thrilled for me and can't wait to meet him and his wife.

After we talked about Ciaro for quite some time, she asked me if I knew what I'm going to do with the rest of the guys. I told her I'm going to let my inner self decide. She's still hoping for a December wedding, even though I told her I'm not so sure it will happen. She remains hopeful anyway. I said I'd be fine with just having a boyfriend for longer than a month when this is over with

⁂

Grams and I decided to go to Red Fox for a light lunch. I could have very easily indulged in wine, but I needed to keep my head clear for the dinner I am about to have. I wish I had the wine at lunch to keep my nerves at bay. I could go to the bar

CHAPTER 5

and order a glass while I wait. I'm a little early and haven't been seated yet.

I look around and I don't see an open spot at the bar. Hell, I don't even see an open table for that matter.

I walk over to the host area. *"Excuse me, I have reservations at six for two, is that going to be running late?"*

"Name?"

"Ciara Verbank."

"I don't see your name written down. Should I put you on the waiting list?"

"No, thanks."

I turn to leave and see him come in. He's not hard to miss with him being as tall as he is. He smiles as soon as he sees me and I do the same.

"Hey!"

"Hey there yourself! You look beautiful as always." He bends to kiss my cheek.

"They messed up, so they don't have our reservation."

"Do you want to wait?"

"We could go somewhere more quiet."

"Sounds good to me. Where shall we go?"

"How about we go to my apartment and order a pizza or something."

"I'd like that. I'll order from Bruno's and pick it up on the way to your place."

"Perfect. I'll stop to get us a bottle of wine."

"I'm looking forward to spending alone time with you."

"I'll see you soon."

I stop at The Liquor Barn to get a bottle of sweet red wine. If I remember correctly, it's one of his favorite wines. The jitters I felt earlier are slowly vanishing. I'm actually glad that our reservations were messed up. I want this private time alone without being surrounded by strangers. If things go wrong, and we do break up, I don't need an audience for it.

I am only at my apartment long enough for me to get wine glasses out and plates for our pizza. It makes me happy when I hear the knock on the door. I go to the door to let him in.

"Hi."

"Hello again."

"The pizza smells good."

He carries the pizza to the kitchen. He sees the bottle of wine I bought.

"Great choice."

"I figured you'd like it."

I open the wine and pour us glasses. We take our

pizza and wine to the living room and make ourselves cozy on the sofa.

"I remember the last time I was here."

"I do too. I remember I woke up and the bed felt cold."

"You looked so peaceful, I didn't want to wake you."

"How is Shay doing?"

"Oh my gosh, my baby is growing too fast before my eyes."

Warrick and I continue talking as we eat and drink the bottle of wine. He's always been so easy to talk with. I adore Shay and love hearing about her. However, the longer we sit here and carry on with small talk, it feels like there's an elephant in the room. I'm not sure he feels as much as I do. He seems to be cool as a cucumber. The evening is going so well, I'm not sure I'm ready to talk about us. I know it needs to be done, I'm just not ready.

The longer we talk the more I know I have to bring up our relationship. I don't think I can hold this in any longer. I am feeling more and more guilty. Sadly, I just don't have the butterflies I once did. I don't have the deep giddy feelings I should just by being with him. I close my eyes and a tear drips down to my cheek. Warrick reaches over to where I am and brings me into his arms. He kisses the top of my head.

"Ciara, it's okay."

"How can you say that? Nothing I am about to do is okay."

"I never thought I could develop feelings for another woman after Shay's mother, but you have shown me it is possible. I will forever be grateful for the time we did have together."

"I feel so bad that I just don't think what we have is what I'm looking for long term. I loved you, Warrick, I really did."

"I believe you." He wipes my cheeks, then lifts my face to look at him. *"I want you to have the kind of love that sets your soul on fire. If I don't do that, there is someone else who will. I adore you to pieces. Breaking up with me in person shows me you are genuine and kind."*

"I wish it was you. I don't want to hurt you."

"Honestly, I wish it were me, too, but it's not. I'm going to be alright, though. I want a woman that loves me as much as I love her. Love is possible for me, it's just not with you."

Warrick holds me as I continue to cry. I want so badly to flip a switch inside me and say you are the one for me. I'd be cheating us both, though. He stays with me long enough for me to dry up my tears. After he leaves, I curl up into a ball and cry some more. I hate this feeling. It saddens me that he just wasn't the man for me. I pray that he finds someone to love. Someone who will love Shay just as equally.

CHAPTER SIX
CIARA

Breaking up with Warrick affected me more than I thought it would. It took me days to get myself back together. Yesterday I opened the journal that Adler gave me and looked at what I had written on the plane. I only wrote the guy's names, that's as far as I got. I then turned the page and started writing about how it felt to break up with an incredible man. By the time I was through, I knew in my heart I did the right thing because I listened to what all of me said and not just what the heart wanted me to feel. When I closed the book, I knew who I needed to see next. As I stand here ready to be face to face with the next guy, I have no way of knowing how it's going to turn out. I wish I did, so that I could prepare myself for more heartache or butterflies floating in my belly.

I reach my hand up to knock on the door and a wave of emotion courses through my veins. I drop my

CHAPTER 6

arm and stand here staring at his door. What if he's with somebody else? I did come here unannounced. I didn't give him any warning that I was coming. What if I made a mistake by coming here today? Ugh! I'm so sick of these goddamn emotions. One minute I'm perfectly fine and the next I feel like I'm going to crumble. Just knock on the damn door, I tell myself.

I lift my hand again. *"Are you going to actually knock this time?"*

I jump back, then spin on my heels. *"You shouldn't sneak up on a girl like that. You scared the hell out of me."*

"Technically, I wasn't sneaking. You just didn't hear my footsteps."

Man he's such a handsome man, standing there with his messy black hair and fuck me eyes. *"You have a habit of being sneaky."*

He laughs. *"I was in the pool room first, if I remember correctly."* He comes closer to me and I get chills. *"Where's your dog?"*

"You mean the one you called a twat? She's home."

"I see." He opens the door and gestures for me to go in first. I step inside. After he closes the door, his hands come around my waist, and he brings my body back to his. I gasp when his hand slides up my body

to my jaw. He turns my head and then kisses me. My heart pumps hard in my chest. *"I have to get ready to race. Are you staying?"*

"Yes," I say with labored breathing.

"Good! You can sit with Carl."

"This is your last race?"

"No, there's one more after today. Next week, I either win the championship or I go home in second place. I have no plan on being second." He kisses me again. *"God you get more beautiful every time I see you."*

"You aren't too shabby yourself, Hawk Evans."

Literally, I think Hawk makes my panties melt. I am definitely attracted to him sexually. I just need to figure out if the rest of what could be us is meant to be.

ૐ

I jump down from the pit box and follow Carl to the garage area. By the time we reach Hawk, he's climbing out of his car. I can see the disappointment written all over his face even though he smiles when he sees me. Winning the championship means the world to him. Today's mishap with the engine doesn't help his chance. I stand back while he gets stopped to do an interview. He keeps sneaking glances at me and I hope nobody catches on. I didn't show up today to be Carl's publicity stunt. I came here today because I wanted to be here to see Hawk race and find out if what we share is real enough to last us a lifetime.

"Well if it isn't the girl who got me fired! What brings you here, Ciara? Is it love or are you here to break poor Hawk's heart?"

"Leave her alone, Bethany. You have no right to butt your nose in my business." He takes my hand, and we start to walk away. *"By the way, you got yourself fired,"* he says to her over his shoulder.

"You didn't need to do that. I could have handled her."

"Bethany would have never listened to you. She would have kept throwing insults at you, getting the last word in."

We reach Hawk's bus and I am surprised when he opens the car door instead of the bus. I get in and I watch him strip from his fire suit tossing it inside. He lets his dog out then comes to get in the car.

"Where are we going?"

"Some place that isn't here."

"Sorry you didn't win today."

"It's the name of the game I guess. It's not over

yet, I still have a shot at winning next week in Arizona."

Hawk drives us around in what felt like we were going in circles. But I don't know this area at all. I got off the plane and went straight to the track. I've never been to Virginia.

My eyes go wide when he pulls into a hotel. *"I thought maybe you'd like to take a swim."*

"You did, did you?"

"Seems like a great idea to me."

We go in and Hawk books a room. We go to the room and as soon as we're inside, he pins me to the wall. His lips are on me in an instant. His hands go for my shirt.

"Can't swim in these clothes."

Breathless I say, *"No we can't."*

He takes all my clothing off and I'm doing absolutely nothing to stop him. I watch as he strips. Damn his body is sculpted like a piece of art. He goes to the bathroom and brings out a robe for me to put on. My confusion must be showing.

"Can't have you walking the halls nude."

"And what about swimming?"

"I can't have my way with you if you have a suit on now can I?"

"Umm…"

CHAPTER 6

"Shh! I have it all figured out."

We leave the room in only a robe. Hawk has got to be the most wild person I know. I admit, I like it.

We reach the pool room and there are people in the water. I am not taking this robe off. Not in his wildest dreams will I be doing that. Hawk walks over to the person on watch duty and chats with him. Next thing I know, he's telling everyone the pool is closing for maintenance. I run my hand across my forehead. This guy is goddamn crazy. He walks back toward me, proud of himself.

"What did you say to him?"

"I told him who I am and asked if he wanted an all-expense paid weekend to next week's race."

I see the people getting out and leaving. *"You are nuts."*

"You love it."

Yes, Hawk, I do! I want to say that to him, but I hold back. I don't need him getting a bigger head than he already has.

Once everyone leaves, Hawk gives a thumbs up to the guy. The lights dim and we are left alone. I still don't know if I'm taking this robe off. Anyone could walk in on us.

"What's stopping anyone from walking in?"

"He locked the door. No one can get in, but we can get out."

Hawk is the definition of bad boy. I feel the tie strap around my waist getting loose. Then his hands on my skin sends shivers down my spine. I can't deny Hawk makes my body respond to his touch. I become putty in his hands. My robe slips off my shoulders and lays on the floor near my feet. I stand here nude, frozen in place.

" I want to see you dive." I take in a deep breath. *"Get in the water, Ciara."*

I move my feet and go to the deep end. I don't think twice about diving in. I swim underwater until I need air. When I come up, I brush my hair back with my hands, then wipe the water off my face. I look at him. What is he waiting for? I float on my back.

"Are you coming?"

He laughs. *"You'll know when I do."*

I roll my eyes, and twist as I push myself under. I swim underwater for as long as I can. Hawk is messing with me. Two can play that game. I come to the top of the water and put my head back. My hair floats. When I pick my head up. I keep my eyes locked on his. I cup my breasts and play with my nipples. I lick my lips. He narrows his lust filled eyes. I turn, putting my back to him. I slide a hand down between my legs and moan. I hear the splash and I swim to the other side. I grab the side of the pool. Hawk is right there behind me.

"Finish what you started." I shake my head no. He takes my hand and puts it between my legs. *"Get yourself off for me."*

I start playing with myself and my head falls backward to his shoulder. My other hand slips off the edge of the pool. As I get myself off, I feel my body floating away from the side. Hawk holds my body up above the water while holding one of my breasts. I add another finger inside me. Getting that much closer to an orgasm. I feel his manhood is hard between our bodies. I want it inside me. I want him to bring my body the pleasure it seeks.

I slip a hand between us, taking his cock in my hand. Then I feel the chill on my skin as Hawk carries me out of the pool. He goes to the darkest corner, putting me to my feet. I feel his absence as he walks away from me. He picks up our robes and brings them back to where I am. He puts mine over my shoulders and I put my arms in the sleeves. He puts his on as well. When he takes my hand, we go to a lounge chair. He sits, stretching out his legs. He takes hold of his shaft and I lick my lips.

"Finish what you started."

I straddle his lap, taking him inside me. I rock my hips back and forth, using him as he said. My nails dig into the skin of his shoulders as I come closer. Hawk holds my hips, moving me fast. I moan out as his cock fills me. I fall forward, no longer able to hold myself up. I orgasm. He groans and my body is no longer under my control. It has fallen under his spell. His arms wrap around my body when his release comes.

※

I had no intention of having sex with Hawk today. I couldn't help myself. I am highly sexually attracted to him. I love his wildness, his personality, and his spontaneity. As we sit in the hotel lounge, I try to figure out if I could see myself with him forever. How does our lives fit with one another? Hawk travels, what, ten months out of the year? Where would my career fit into his lifestyle? I understand race car drivers have successful marriages. I just don't understand how they do it.

"What are you thinking about?"

"How long do you plan on racing?"

"Until I'm old and can't get in and out of a car anymore." He smiles. I roll my eyes. *"Honestly, I*

don't know. Right now, racing is like a drug and I need it. Some day I assume I won't need it as much as my attention will be on other things."

"How do you see family life fitting into your life right now?"

"You want me to be completely honest, right?"

"I do."

"I wasn't looking for a relationship, then you came along. I didn't think I could want something other than being behind a wheel of a fast car. You proved me wrong. I haven't been with anyone since I met you. I want you. Someday I would want to have a family, but I'm not ready for that yet. I'm not fully sure I'm ready for marriage."

"I'm not sure I'm ready, either. How do you see us in a relationship with your traveling?"

"I guess we'd have to live it as a couple to figure it out. I know your business is as important to you as racing is to me." He reaches over and puts his hand over top of mine. *"I'm all in if you are. I'm crazy about you, Ciara. I wasn't looking for love, but I found it when I met you."*

"I am crazy about you, too. You make me get so far out of my comfort zone and it makes me feel so alive. It scares me when the adrenaline wears off, we will crash into a wall."

"I have fears too, but nothing like yours. Yours makes me feel like we are doomed before we even get our feet off the ground."

"What are your fears?"

"That I'm not good enough for you." He takes his hand away. *"I think you just proved what I feared most."*

"I didn't mean to make you feel that way. It's not true, you are good enough for me. I'm sorry if that came out wrong. I am having a difficult time figuring out how I am going to split my life in half to be with you."

"Ciara, if I'm not the right guy for you, I'll eventually find a woman who I am right for. I love you, but if you are having this many doubts about us, then that should be red flags."

I cover my face with my hands. I try to hold the tears back, but it doesn't work. How can I feel this pull toward him and still have these reservations? He's right, I do have too many doubts. But, damn it, he fills my insides with butterflies.

"I am going to make this easy on you." He takes my hands away from my face. He uses his thumb to wipe my eyes. Then he leans in and kisses me. *"You, Ciara Verbank, are an interesting, sexy lady that I fell for. I have no regrets being with you. I love you."*

He kisses my cheek. Before I can say anything to him, he gets up and leaves me sitting here alone. I want to run after him, but something deep inside me says don't do it. The tears come on heavier. I feel like a piece of shit. Hawk and I did have a connection. It was real. Sadly, I couldn't see how it would be a lasting relationship. If I end up alone after all of this, I deserve it.

CHAPTER SEVEN
CIARA

I felt destroyed when Hawk left. I was left feeling like I lost the man for me. I am so very confused. How can chemistry be that strong between two people and we end up broken up? It happened so fast. We went from hot and heavy to ice cold in a blink of an eye. I was left with the sense that no relationship is going to work. I didn't know what to do. I was left alone in Virginia in a hotel bar. I wished I was anywhere but there. I wanted someone to comfort me and tell me everything was going to be okay. I wanted Porter. Porter is never going to leave me.

I left the hotel and went to a twenty-four hour cafe. I needed a cup of tea and a quiet place to think. I sat in that cafe and I couldn't get any of my thoughts straight. I was barely holding myself together. All I wanted to do was cry. I eventually broke and did in fact cry. I sat there blubbering like a fool. I needed someone to talk to, so I called Porter. He did make me feel better. Well at least good enough so that I stopped crying. I ended up leaving the cafe and checked into a different hotel. I went right to my room, collapsing on the bed. I laid there, staring at the ceiling. I thought about what Porter told me on the phone. If Hawk was the one for me, I would have chased after him and refused to let him go. Porter also told me that when I'm face to face with my true love, I'm going to know it. If that is true, how did I walk away the first time? Wouldn't I have told Grams I already found the man of my dreams?

I went to sleep that night feeling defeated. I said a silent prayer that I didn't waste the last ten months of my life. I want what Ciaro and Molena have so badly, I can almost taste it. I'm starving for it at this point.

Today I woke up feeling the same as I did when I went to sleep. I feel like a piece of me died last night. As I wait to leave Virginia, I think about how horrible I feel. I want this pain to go away. I don't want to see the hurt on any more faces, either. I am tempted to tell Grams I am not strong enough to hold this storm in my hands. I want her to tell the remainder of the guys I am done, that I am ending it with every single one of them. That isn't the adult thing to do, though. I have to be the one who faces these wonderful men and hurt them.

I hear the flight boarding, so I gather my things and hope I get my shit together before my plane lands. I wish this month never came. No, I wish I wasn't a cruel human being. I am just a horrible person deep down and I deserve to feel this way.

CHAPTER EIGHT
CIARA

The first thing I did when I landed was check into a room. Then I went for a walk outside for well over an hour. I'm not feeling any better about myself, but the fresh air feels nice. I found a place to sit and let the sun shine on my face. I sent a couple text messages to Lincoln and he's coming to meet me. I wasn't sure if he was in LA or New York, I took a chance and came here. I consider myself lucky I guessed right.

As I sit here and wait, my hopes of finding love is at a zero for me. I decided that I'm not going to do the whole date thing with Lincoln. I'm just going to be blunt with him. I can't sit through the entire day with him looking for something that isn't there. Lincoln is a fabulous man. Any woman would be lucky to be his. He has a heart of gold and deserves to have one equal to his. My heart is not gold. It's probably black and rotten to the core.

I feel a hand on my shoulder. *"Ciara, are you alright?"*

"Not really."

Lincoln comes around the wooden bench and sits beside me. He puts an arm around me and I come unglued.

"Let it out, sweetheart."

"I've never felt this kind of pain before."

"Sometimes we need pain for growth."

"I don't want to grow then. My little bubble I was in, I was just fine."

"Let's go back to my place. I don't live far."

I nod my head. I wipe my cheeks with the sleeve of my sweater. As we walk to his car, I keep my head down. I can't look anyone in the eyes, even strangers. In the car, I bury my face in my hands.

"I'm sorry."

"You have nothing to be sorry for."

"Yes I do. I'm a fucking wreck. I can't think straight at all."

Lincoln takes my hands from my face. I turn to look away. He holds one of my hands as he drives us. I lean my head on the window and cry more. He shouldn't be showing me his kindness. He does know

CHAPTER 8

I'm about to break up with him? If he doesn't, I'm going to crush his hopes.

Lincoln was right, he doesn't live far. He helps me out of the car like the gentleman he is. We get to his door and I freeze. I can't find the strength to step inside. Lincoln lifted me off my feet, cradling me in his arms. He lays me out on his sofa, then covers me with a blanket. He sits beside me, bending to kiss my forehead.

"I'm going to give you privacy. You need rest." His hand cups my face. *"Cry if that's what you need to do. No judgment here."* He kisses my forehead again before standing.

I grab his hand and sit up. *"I don't want to be alone."*

Because Lincoln is who is, he sits by the arm of the sofa and I lay my head on his lap. He doesn't say a word, but him brushing my hair with his hand relaxes me. I don't stop crying fully, but it isn't a full-blown cry either. I close my eyes and feel myself drifting. I feel safe with him.

I woke up and for a moment I forgot where I was. Lincoln has left me to sleep alone. The way he comforted me, was something I needed. I am mentally and physically exhausted. I could sleep for days and it probably wouldn't phase me.

I get off the sofa and look around. Across the room, I see Lincoln outdoors on the balcony. His carpet is soft under my feet. I peek my head out. He has his nose buried in a newspaper.

"Hi."

I startled him. *"Hi. How are you feeling?"*

I shrug my shoulders because I don't really know how I am feeling. There are so many emotions inside me that I don't know which one is the strongest.

"How long have I been asleep? It feels like it got warmer."

"You fell asleep yesterday." What? No way have I been out that long. *"Do you want some tea, coffee, juice?"*

"I've really been out that long? You should have woken me up."

"You must have needed the rest and I wasn't about to wake you."

I come outside, sitting next to him and bring my knees to my chest. *"Thank you, Lincoln."*

CHAPTER 8

"You are welcome. You can stay as long as you wish. And I'm here to lend a shoulder, an ear to listen, and do whatever it is you need me to do for you."

"Hey, you know that wedding we went to? Cora's best friend."

"Yes, I remember."

"Cora and Asher are doing another movie together and I was asked to do their wardrobe."

"That's excellent news."

"Ya it was pretty cool. Thank you for taking me to that wedding. If you hadn't I would not have met Cora."

"You are very welcome."

Lincoln gets up and tells me he'll be right back. I stand myself and walk over to the railing and take in a deep breath. When he comes back, he sets a cup of tea down and wraps a blanket around my shoulders. I join him back at sitting beside each other.

"I thought a lot about our relationship after you left. In many ways we became very good friends. The romantic relationship was slower to come along. I developed feelings for you."

"I..." he cuts me off.

"Please let me finish."

"Okay."

"My feelings for you were very real. However, I

see a lot of people in love. I realized that maybe your feelings weren't where mine were. I want you to know, it's okay if you didn't share what I felt. That's just a part of life. If I can't have you as a girlfriend or wife, I want us to at least be friends."

I take his hand. *"I don't think I got to the point of loving you the way a man should be loved. I care very deeply for you. I would want you to remain in my life as a friend."*

My eyes well up with tears. *"Don't feel bad, okay? I have absolutely no regrets taking a chance on love. I received love, just not the romantic kind. I cherish what we shared. I hope we have many days ahead of us as friends."*

I felt a little bit of weight lifted off my shoulders. I still feel like a horrible person though.

"I'd love to make many more memories with you."

"You can talk to me, Ciara. If you are confused about your other relationships, I might be able to help you sort out your feelings."

"I already broke it off with three other guys. The last one gutted me. We had a strong chemistry toward one another, but it ended. It just confuses me about my feelings for the rest of the men. I feel sick that I *hurt this much and even worse because I know I hurt someone more than I hurt myself."*

"*Love isn't always as clear as we think. Strong chemistry can be deceiving. Yes you can be sexually attracted to somebody, but you need to be emotionally connected as well. You get what I am saying?"*

"*It makes sense when it's said that way."*

What Lincoln is saying is making sense to me. It's just confusing to recognize the two differences. I do believe I loved Hawk, maybe I just didn't see or want to see that we are in two different places in life. I think Hawk had real feelings for me as well. Maybe our love story's timing was just all wrong. He still wants to live the Nasar driver life, and I wasn't ready to give up my own career to travel with him. Maybe we just didn't love each other enough to compromise.

"*You have feelings for more than one guy, right?"*

"*Yes."*

"*You have been on a long journey. When you come to stand before the man you love deeper than the rest, you'll know. You feel with your heart, Ciara, it's not going to let you down."*

"*Thanks for saying that."*

"*You've got to remember, each one of us guys signed up for this. We all took our chances just as you did for us. We knew we could get hurt and we all still did it. If we hurt, it's for our own growth."*

"You, Lincoln Titus, are too wise."

"I don't know everything, but I try to think logically."

Lincoln has made me feel better about myself. I'm still torn up, but not as bad as I was. I truly hope these guys don't stop looking for love, they all deserve it.

CHAPTER NINE
CIARA

I spent two days at Lincoln's. Well, technically three, but I spent the first day sleeping away. Once Lincoln basically let me off the hook for breaking up with him, I did feel a sense of relief. He could tell I was still struggling with my feelings. He didn't ask for intimate deals of my other relationship, but he let me discuss the details I wanted to give. Talking to him helped get my head on straighter. I'm still a bit emotional, but not such the emotional wreck I was when arriving. His advice to me was basically the same as my father gave me, listen to what my soul tells me is right. From here on out, I hope I can do that. I thought I was doing that with Hawk, but it backfired. Lincoln's opinion on that is I was blinded by the sexual gravity. If Hawk was truly the one for me, I would have never let it fall apart in a blink of an eye. I also wouldn't have shown up to him so quickly, either because I would have gone after Hawk. I have to take what he says as truth. Hawk and I just weren't meant to be a lasting couple.

I'm scared to death to go off to see where the next relationship will go. I'm leaving my mind open and being cautious with my heart. If I'm not cautious, I might lead myself to another breakdown. I can't go back to that place. I don't think I'll be able to pull myself together another time.

🍂

I don't know where I got the strength to get on another flight, but here I am back on the ground in another state. I didn't call ahead, send a text or anything so I am showing up out of the blue. It's probably a little foolish to just show up like this, but it is what it is. It's how I wanted to do this.

I rented a car and drove for quite some time. I forgot how long it takes to drive there. As I head up the hill that made me nervous the last time I was here, it doesn't seem to bother me this time. My nerves are preoccupied dealing with other matters.

When I pull into the driveway I see his vehicles right away. I feel the air from my lungs disappear. I sit here with the engine running, telling myself I got this.

CHAPTER 9

It's time to either end another relationship or build one with a soft hearted man. With the way our relationship ended, it can go either way. As I said earlier, I'm being cautious.

I eventually turn the car off and work up the strength to get out and knock on his door. When he doesn't answer my heart pounds harder in my chest. I let out the puff of air I was holding in. With a shaky hand, I try the door handle and it isn't locked. Peeking my head inside, I call out his name. I get no reply. Stepping off of the porch, I walk around to the side of the house and look around. It's still beautiful here, even with all the leaves on the ground. His home is definitely one of my favorite places. I take one look at the rental and then I start walking. I'm pretty sure I know where I can find him.

I didn't remember just how far this would be to go by foot. I am no longer out of breath from nerves. My lungs are burning from the hike. It's a beautiful day, so it's worth it. The air is crisp and even though the leaves hang around in its colors on the ground, the smell of fall is gone.

"Ciara?"

I hear my name and I spin in a circle. I don't know where his voice came from. Maybe I was hearing things. Taking a seat on the bench, I feel disappointed I didn't find him. I thought for sure he'd be right here.

"That was you I saw! What on earth are you doing?"

When he asks what I am doing here my heart skips a beat. Does he not want me here? I twist on the bench and see Kirby dressed in camouflage behind me.

"I went to the house first but you weren't there. I'm sorry, I guess I should have told you I was coming."

"You don't need an invitation to my house."

"It kinda sounds that way when you ask what on earth am I doing here."

"Sorry, you took me by surprise. It's hunting season. You could get yourself hurt."

"Oh!" I guess that would explain the camouflage and the crossbow in his hand.

"I'm happy to see you."

I cannot control myself and burst out loud laughing. It's hard to take him seriously with his handsome face covered in paint.

"I'm sorry, but you look, umm…"

"Handsome, right!"

"Yea, we'll go with that. You kinda smell like piss or something like that."

CHAPTER 9

"I suppose I would. I should probably shower. You can ride with me down to the house."

"I think I want to walk."

"That's not happening, sweetheart! My dad is still in the woods hunting."

"Oh! I better not end up smelling like you!"

"My shower is big enough for two." He nudged my shoulder with his. *"I'm kidding. I'll take my jacket off so you don't stink like fox piss."*

※

Kirby comes out into the main part of his house in only a pair of sweatpants. Damn, damn, damn! I bite my bottom lip to stop the words about to slip out. He has a seat on the sofa that I'm on. He looks at me, then uses his thumb to pull my lip from my teeth.

"Umm, Porter, I'll call you later."

I hang up the phone and put it aside.

"I have to admit I'm pretty surprised by you being here. Our last day together didn't end so well, then you ignored my calls for days."

"You're not beating around the bush."

"My mother taught me to be upfront and don't let the elephant sit in the room too long."

"I see."

"Are you here to break up with me or take our relationship to the next step?"

"What if I told you I don't know the answer to that?"

"What else could I say besides take your time and figure it out who is right for you."

"We spent a whole month together and I feel I didn't give you all of me. I held back on a lot, that is why I wanted to bring you to my place."

"That's why you were so angry with me?"

"Yes. I wanted to make it up to you."

"Ciara, if you think I shared everything there is about who I am with you in one month, I'm here to tell you I haven't."

"Tell me something I don't know about you."

"I fear I won't be a good husband because of my career choice."

"I fear I will be a horrible mother because my mother left me."

Kirby touches my cheek. *"Your heart's too big for you to ever be a horrible mother. That much I know about you."*

"You, Mr. Rhodes are going to be a wonderful husband because you were raised with your mother's values to love all things around you."

CHAPTER 9

"I want to go back to our last night together and listen to whatever you want to tell me about what you think I should know."

I begin to tell Kirby about my childhood and how I was raised and how it made me feel growing up. I end up telling him a little about my dating history, especially about Hunter and why everyone was so worried. We talk for hours. Well, I did most of the talking and he listened, soaking up whatever I wanted to tell him. I feel better letting him into parts of my life that I didn't share with him back in August. I know I didn't tell him every aspect of who I am, but it's more than what I gave him before. After I was all talked out, Kirby shared more with me about his fears about being a husband and a father. I learned he wants all that, but can't figure out how it will work out.

I look at my phone when Kirby gets up to get us another drink. I can't believe it's almost eleven at night. We talked so long we missed dinner and the stars replaced the sun. I feel this is a good place to call it a night.

Kirby hands me the glass of wine. I set it on the table. *"Something the matter?"*

"Earlier you asked me if I was here to break up with you or go to the next."

He smiles his ever so handsome smile. *"I do remember that."*

"Things have ended with four of the guys already."

"I see."

"I feel like I need more time to think. I have other relationships I must work through before I can give you an answer."

Kirby drinks his entire glass of wine in one big sip. It's probably not right by me asking him to wait longer for my decision. I feel it's the right choice to make right this second for me. I'm not ready to call it quits or say he's the one. I just don't know yet. I can't be more honest than that.

"If you need more time I'm going to tell you to take it. I'll wait for your answer."

I lean into his space and kiss him. *"Thank you."*

We say our goodbyes and I feel a hundred percent happy with how I left things. It might have been the most adult thing I've done in a while.

CHAPTER TEN
CIARA

I stayed in a very quaint hotel last night in town. It would have been nice if I could have stayed on the reservation but, an hour drive was not something I wanted to do. This morning I would have loved to fly home, but I set off to figure out another relationship. I am going in just as I did with Kirby. Being open minded and cautious with my heart seemed to work, so I'm going to do my best to do it again. I have had a lot of unknowns these past eleven months, today is no different. I long for a day that I don't have to walk in blind anymore.

I hand my ticket to the attendant, then follow the people in front of me. As I do, I feel like I am the only person that is alone. It's a feeling that I do not like at all. I see couples of all ages holding hands, sharing a kiss, or simply enjoying the company of the person they're with. I have that hunger inside me. Although I want to fill that void, I still have tiny doubts trying to overpower hope. If I had a magic wand or could see the future, all this would be over with. Since I don't my future still is up in the air.

I make my way through the crowd just as the lights dim. When Jasper comes out on stage, I think back to the first time we met and how I turned to putty in his hands. What he did on that plane makes my body tingle. I know that Jasper and I have a strong sexual bond. This time I am not going to let that interfere like I did with Hawk. I need to know if there is an emotional connection as well. I need to know if there is more to us than sex and good conversation. Would Jasper be husband material for me is what I'm going to find out.

I am surrounded by Jasper's fans. He lives a lifestyle I'm not sure I could handle. Like Hawk, he travels a great deal. Months at a time he leaves his home in Tennessee and lives on a tour bus. That doesn't leave much time for family life. I already established I don't want this lifestyle. I am not ready to give up my career. I don't think I could handle the way women throw themselves at him either. It's almost like Hawk and Jasper are cut from the same cloth. Their lives are glamorous and in the spotlight.

CHAPTER 10

I'm not that kind of person. I am much more low key.

I feel my cheeks blushing the moment Jasper's eyes lock on mine. Why does he have to be sex on legs? No wonder the ladies are gaga over him, I am too. I have to remind myself I am looking for a long term relationship and not just hot sex.

I feel a tap on my shoulder. I look and it's Jasper's security team. I look back at Jasper and he nods his head. I'm guessing I'm supposed to leave with them. I wanted to see the concert, but this is best so that I can be taken backstage or to his tour bus.

When you are enjoying yourself, I guess time slips by without much knowledge. I hadn't realized Jasper was already on stage for over an hour when I left with the security guys. After we made our way through the crowd, I was quickly being led toward the tour bus. I could faintly hear Jasper saying goodbye to his fans. I am let inside his bus and told he'll be right here.

Only like ten minutes have passed when the door opens. He tosses his cowboy hat on the counter.

"What a pleasant surprise. You should have told me you were coming, I would have gotten you in."

"It was a last minute decision."

He sits next to me. *"How long are you here for?"*

"I have a flight to catch at five."

"In the morning?"

"Yes."

"That doesn't give us much time."

"I know."

"So the moment has finally come, huh?"

"It has."

"The suspense is killing me. What have you decided?"

"I haven't decided anything yet."

"I see."

"It's been a long year. I am trying to weed through my feelings still."

"What are you questioning about us?"

"Our lifestyles are different. I don't know if I am able to become a traveling girlfriend."

"My tour ends next week. I have already told the guys I'm taking time off. I want to spend more time on the ranch and write. I'm tired of all the travel."

"Was I part of that decision?"

"It helped push me toward it, yes, but I've been wanting this for a while. Life on the road isn't easy. I'm exhausted, if I'm being honest. I feel I am losing myself in all the fame."

"What happens after you write and take time off?"

CHAPTER 10

"You mean in a year from now if I'll go back on the road?"

"Yes."

"If I do it will be short. I can't go back to being on tour for over a year." He takes my hand. *"One morning I looked in the mirror and I didn't recognize myself. I could see the change in my face of what being a star did to me. I looked stressed, tired, and unhappy. You have that look."*

"I am definitely stressed and tired. This journey has taken a toll on me. I developed feelings for everyone for different reasons and ways. I'm trying my damndest to work everything out."

"I fell in love with you. There's no doubt in my mind about it. I'm not interested in anyone else. I have been waiting for you to come, but I was hoping it was to tell me I'm the one."

"I wish I could tell you that you are but I'm just not there yet. I have to sort through all these emotions. I want no regrets by the time I decide what I want to do."

"Are you questioning anything besides my career?"

"If I want to be with you, are you looking for marriage?"

"I'm not looking to get married next month. Even-

tually, I want to be a family man. I don't feel there should be a deadline as Millie gave."

"A wedding next month seems unrealistic, but people do it and make it last."

"That they do, I guess. Want to get out of here? Grab a late dinner?"

I lean into his space and kiss him. Jasper deepens the kiss. With his lips on mine, I want to rip his clothes off. I wipe his lips with my thumb. A wave of emotions comes over me. I sit here staring into his eyes. Jasper is a good guy. I love him.

"Actually, I think I should go."

"Where are you going?"

"Not sure."

"Did I do something wrong?" I turn my head away, I can't look at him. *"When I saw you in the mix of my fans, it instantly made me happy. A feeling of having you in my sight gave me chills. It's indescribable, actually. I don't do that for you, do I?"*

"Jasper, you give me feelings of excitement whenever I see you. I don't know if it's lust or love. I wish I could figure it out. At this time I can't decipher which one it is."

"Are you asking me to wait around until you figure it out?"

Tears fill my eyes. *"I don't think I am."*

He gets off the couch we've been sitting on and takes the few steps it takes to be in the kitchen. I can see the hurt he's feeling. I hate that I caused it.

"I can't imagine what it's been like to walk in your shoes the past ten months with so many men. I do understand how everything can be confusing for you. I'm not confused at all. I want a life with you. I fell in love."

"I'm sorry that I don't know."

"If you get to a point of knowing and figure out I'm more than lust, I'll be in Tennessee."

He opens a drawer and takes out something. He brings it to me. I take it.

"What is this?"

"A song I wrote about loving one person. I wrote it for you."

I get up with tears streaming down my face. Jasper pulls me to him and his scent fills my nose. I am flooded with guilt or grief. Maybe it's a new kind of sadness. Whatever it is, it doesn't feel good. I don't fully know why I told him not to wait for me. I could very well have made a mistake.

CHAPTER ELEVEN
CIARA

I changed my flight to an earlier time. I also changed my destination. I was ready to go to Vegas, but I decided I need to go somewhere else first. The problem with that, I don't know where that is. So, I came back to the city. Instead of going home to Grams', I went to Porter's. He has something of mine that I needed. I didn't stay there, I left only after an hour of being there and went to my apartment. Porter tried to get me to stay and get some sleep. I appreciate his offering, but I wanted to be alone.

This morning I woke up and went for a walk to get some coffee. I don't normally drink it because I prefer tea. However, I do enjoy a strong flavorful Hazelnut coffee every now and then. I wasn't really hungry, so I skipped getting anything to eat. It's probably not a healthy decision since I haven't been eating very much lately.

CHAPTER 11

On the plane ride home, I thought about the breakup with Jasper. I was proud of myself for not giving in to temptation. Let's face it the man is fucking sexy and he knows it. I could have very easily hopped into his bed. Lord knows it crossed my mind a few times watching him on stage. It all boiled down to I wasn't there to have hot passionate sex. Sitting on his bus talking to him, I realized my inner self was talking to me. I felt Jasper and I just weren't going to work. Jasper is a country singer at heart, I don't think I can compete with that. He says he wants family life, and maybe that's true. The man I see is a man who loves the stage. He lights up singing his songs for his fans. If I am wrong, I guess that proves that I just don't know him like I think I do. I want nothing but the best for him. I hope he finds a woman who will love all of him and sticks by his side as he sorts out his roots and his fame.

I settle on the sofa and take a sip of my coffee that is now only lukewarm. I press the video chat button on my phone and hold my breath. I smile when he answers.

"Ciara," he says my name with his amazing smile, *"how are you?"*

"I'm doing, okay. How are you?"

"I'm doing better now that I get to see your beautiful face."

"I have something to show you." I call Alaska over and show Malcolm. "She's growing so fast."

"That she has."

I put her down. "Where are you?"

"I am in Australia."

"Oh!" I look away from a second. "What are you doing there?"

"This is where a lot of my big clients are. I am helping them with a huge security problem if they don't get it fixed."

"I see. How long will you be gone?"

"If I'm not back for Thanksgiving, my mom will have my ass."

"Will you be back by then?"

"It's my plan. I'll have to bust my ass and work long hours." I drink some of my coffee. "Something is eating at you, what is it?"

"Alaska and I were going to come see you."

"You can come as soon as I'm back. I miss you very much."

"I'll have to do that."

"Maybe you would like to come with me to my parents for dinner?"

"We'll see."

"I know it's November and I know what that means."

Here it goes, here comes the waterworks. *"I don't mean to cry. I was really looking forward to seeing you."*

"Sorry, this job came up unexpectedly. It's big, Ciara, or I'd jump on a plane right now and come to you."

"I understand."

"Where are you at?"

"My apartment."

"Are you going to be there all day?"

"Why are you magically going to snap your fingers and be here?"

"I wish."

"I don't know. I might go break..." I stop the rest of that sentence from slipping out.

"Were you coming to break it off with me? I could totally see why you would. I thought it'd be a long shot if we ended up together."

"A long shot? Why would you think that?"

"Because we dated ten months ago. Feelings fade."

"Did your feelings fade for me?"

"No, my heart still beats for you."

"I wasn't sure which way our relationship would

go once we face each other. I'm still sorting that out."

"Are you saying I still have a shot at winning your love?"

"Yeah, I guess I am."

"Baby, you just made my day so much better." God his smile lights up my heart. *"You just gave me even more reason to wrap this job up in a hurry. I want to see you as soon as I get back."*

"I'd like that."

"Oh, before I forget. I got a call a couples days ago about the fire at my place."

"Did they find out who did it?"

"They did. It was some young kids. They weren't targeting me, just out randomly setting fires. They got caught lighting another one few blocks from mine. It was the third place they hit."

"Wow, that's horrible."

"It is. I feel better knowing you don't have to worry or wonder anymore."

"Ya, me too." I hear his video chat making noises. *"What is that?"*

"My mom. She's calling me to remind me to get my ass home. Her daily call."

"It's important to her."

"It's important to me too. I really want to see you."

I smile. *"I want to see you too."*

There's a knock on the door. *"You better get that. My feelings still stand firm for you. I love you, Ciara."*

I blink and the call goes dead. What the hell! I toss my phone, irritated he has done it again. Why does he do that!?

Nobody knows I'm here, so I almost ignore the knocking. I get up to answer the door after the person knocks again. Apparently, they are persistent.

I open to find a person holding a big bouquet of red roses. I take them and then he hands me a box. I thank him and shut my door. Porter is the only person who knows I'm here, so getting a delivery is surprising. I don't think he'd send me flowers.

I open the card. *Ciara, I wish I was with you. Love, Malcolm.*

How on earth did he do this? Christ, the man is in another country. I open the box and I feel giddy inside. I take one of the chocolate covered strawberries out and bite into it. It's heavenly. I get my phone and text him.

Me: Thank you so much for making my day brighter.

Malcolm: You are very welcome.

Me: Can't wait to see you.

Malcolm: That is why I need to work. Go and break up with your other boyfriends so that I am the last man standing.

I put my phone down and get another strawberry. Malcolm sure knows how to put a smile on my face. Whenever I'm around him or talk to him, I don't feel any stress. Malcolm makes me happy.

I want to be happy and stay in this bliss, but I still have relationships hanging in the wind. As much as I don't want to hurt another person, I know I still have three men waiting on me to give them an answer. I guess I'll book another flight for today. The sooner I get this over with, the sooner I can return to being happy.

CHAPTER TWELVE
CIARA

I couldn't get a flight out last night. The earliest I could get was six this morning. It was actually really nice having a night to myself in my apartment. I slept great knowing that happiness was in my heart. I have to say, Malcolm could be the one for me. He just makes everything calm inside. I never feel like the weight of the world is on my shoulders whenever we talk. Malcolm would make a wonderful life partner. He already told me he can run his business anywhere, so maybe I wouldn't have to give up my store and start over elsewhere. The man gave me a puppy for Christ sakes. It's like we already have a child together.

I get out of the cab and stare at the neon lights. It wasn't that long ago I was here with Kirby. I can remember how it made me feel. I didn't like it one bit.

The cab driver gives me my bag. I take it and walk inside. Seven Jewels Casino and Hotel really is a gorgeous place to stay. Gaetano should be proud to have built such a lovely place for himself. I go right to the desk to check-in. I am sure he knows I will be staying here. Gaetano is the type of man that pays attention. The desk clerk gives me my room key and before I can turn around, I can feel his presence.

"Hello, Ciara."

"Hello, Gaetano."

"May I take you to your room."

"I'd be honored."

Gaetano gets my bag from my arm. We head toward the hall to the elevators. I see the eyes of ladies on him as we walk side by side. Gaetano is an attractive man. Ladies would be foolish not to look. He carries himself very well. Almost mysteriously. Unlike those women, I know this man. He is a little mysterious, but overall he's a kind, caring, and a funny man. He knows how to let loose once he's not running his empire.

"Your room, Ma'am."

I reach out and touch his tie. *"Why thank you, Sir."*

I go into my room and he stays at the door. *"I

have to know are you here to see me or are you with someone?"

"I'm here to see you."

"I'll let you get settled in. We could have a late lunch if you'd like?"

"I'd like that a lot."

"I'll come get you in about an hour. Does that work?"

"It does."

He closes the door and I plop down on the bed. I look around the room. Being in Vegas gives me chills. I can't figure out if it's good or bad. Something definitely feels different whenever I am here. Maybe I'm over thinking and it's nothing to be concerned about. I just can't put my finger on if it is because I belong here or if I should run and never look back.

The last time I was here, all I could think about was Kaiden. I was so worried he'd see me with Kirby. This time, when I see him I may break things off with him. I don't know how I feel about him anymore. I was in love with him and I don't know if that changed. I won't until I see him face to face. Right now, though, I need to pull myself together. I'm here to make a decision about Gaetano. I know I had a hard time separating Kaiden and Gaetano from one another. I might not have given Gaetano the full chance to prove to me he could be the one. That is why I came to see him first.

I fall back on the bed and stare up at the ceiling. Twin brothers was not fair to me. I can't be mad at Grams, she didn't know. I made it through my time with both of them, I just really have to listen to what my heart wants and what my head tells me, hope I don't screw this up.

Just a little bit before Gaetano came to get me, I freshened up and changed my clothes. I thought we'd have lunch at the hotel's restaurant or lounge. I was surprised when we left and came to a restaurant. He said that way there would be no interruptions.

As we sit here looking at the menu, I can't help myself from peeking over the top of the menu, catching a glimpse of him. What I see is bothersome. Gaetano is not Kaiden, but the similarity is there. It's like I'm looking at Kaiden but see a different man altogether. The only difference looks wise is Gaetano has a little bit of graying. The two of them have similar personalities, but carry different views on life. I would say Kaiden is the more stubborn one.

CHAPTER 12

Gaetano is more professional. He holds himself to high standards. Don't get me wrong Kaiden is very by the book when it comes to his private club. Gaetano has to have every aspect of his hotel and casino meet his high standards. Kaiden is okay letting others have responsibilities. I don't even know if I'm making any sense to myself. I am trying really hard to not compare the two of them.

"Have you decided what you'd like?"

Oh, umm," I glance at the menu and scan the menu real quick. *"Think I'm going to get the Cranberry Chicken salad."* That isn't something I would ever order, but hey, it might be good.

"Would you like a drink? I know they don't have fruity cocktails, but they have a decent wine list."

"Wine would be nice."

He nods his head and the waitress comes right over. Gaetano orders for the both of us. Before she leaves, she calls him by name. I must show my curiosity.

"She used to work for me."

"I see."

"How have you been?"

"Honestly, some days I feel like the world is crumbling around me and others I am doing alright. This whole experience has taken a toll on me."

"I can see how this whole thing could be complicated. I just hope you are taking care of yourself."

"I'm trying."

The waitress comes with our glasses of wine. The way she looks at him, I'd say she has a crush on Gaetano. I wonder just how closely they worked together. I don't feel it's my place to ask, though.

"Thank you for joining me for lunch."

"Thank you for inviting me."

I try the wine Gaetano ordered. I usually get a sweet flavor. It isn't bad, but I still prefer the sweet over dry.

"Yesterday I was thinking about you and here you are today."

"What were you thinking?"

"The way things ended between us. I almost wish I didn't take you to my father's for dinner."

"It was an odd night. I want you to know that I don't have any hard feelings toward your father."

"What about me?"

"I am not basing our relationship on that night, if that is what you want to know."

"The way I sent you away, I could see why if you did. It wasn't very manly of me to have you leave upset. I should have dealt with everything better."

"As I could have too. I was..." I stop myself from finishing the statement.

"Defending Kaiden. I get that on some level."

"I might have been butting my nose into something that might not have been my business to stick in."

"That's not fully true. You care about my brother. Defending him, that says a lot about who you are. I like that you are protective over those you love."

The silence falls between us. I simply don't know how to reply to what he just said. I drink my wine and hope our food comes soon. This awkwardness isn't what I had in mind for lunch. I wish Kaiden's name didn't get brought up.

"How long are you here for?"

"A day or two. I have more relationships to figure out."

"That's why you came to see me?"

"Yes. I'm not going to lie. I am unsure what my decision is."

"I'm not sure what that means for me. You are hoping today will give you clarity on our relationship?"

"It's what I'm looking for, yes."

Our food arrives and I'm not hungry anymore. I feel like Gaetano has put me in my place or put me on the spot. Coming here is awkward enough for me. Dating brothers was wrong on many, many levels. I feel like Gaetano has been cheated and it's all my fault. It's not my fault though. It's not my fault I fell in love with his brother first.

It hits me like a ton of bricks. Gaetano isn't the man for me. He never was. I was never going to let him prove to me he could be. My feelings for Kaiden are too strong to cross that line. If I met him first, it might have been different. If I met Gaetano first, I might never have fallen for Kaiden at all. I hate this. I have to sit here and tell him he isn't right for me.

"You look like you just saw a ghost or the answer just came to you."

"I..." He cuts me off.

"I'm a smart guy, Ciara. I live in the real world most of the time. I envy the man who ends up with you."

"I didn't say anything."

"You don't need to. Even if you don't see it, I do."

"See what?"

"You may care about me, but you aren't in love with me."

"I do care about you and I feel if things were different, I could have fallen in love with you."

"One thing I always wished is that I met you first.

I knew dating me after him gave me a disadvantage right off the bat."

"I don't know what to say besides I'm sorry. Grams didn't know you were brothers."

"You have nothing to be sorry for. You were blindsided in more ways than one."

"That is true, but it doesn't make this any easier for me or you."

"I wish nothing but the best for you, Ciara. You are an amazing woman and I truly hope you find love."

"Even if it's with Kaiden?"

"Yes. I assume you haven't seen him?"

"I haven't."

"Neither have I."

"Have either of you tried?"

"No. I'm not sure us being twins means anything past the fact we were born the same day."

"That's a shame."

"It is, but time isn't healing any old wounds."

I look at my lunch. Neither one of us has touched our food. I can't even think about putting that salad in my stomach.

Gaetano touches my shoulder. *"If you ever need a friend to chase you to Jamaica, let me know."* I laugh.

"I'm serious. I want us to be friends. I care very deeply for you."

I was doing so well with not tearing up. *"I'd like that."*

"Good. As a friend, I'm telling you, you need to eat."

"This salad isn't anything I'd eat."

"I have just the thing you need."

Gaetano pays the bill and we leave. He takes me back to the hotel's restaurant where we indulged in the dessert bar. Sweets is what I needed. I feel the change between us. I think we can be friends.

CHAPTER THIRTEEN
CIARA

Gaetano had to attend to a problem in one of the rooms. He walked me back to my room before he left me. I sat in the room staring at the four walls, driving myself crazy. I grabbed my purse and went down to the casino. I didn't really care if I won or lost, I just wanted a distraction. There's this fire burning inside me to find Kaiden. However, I am trying to contain myself and wait until tomorrow. I'm finding it difficult to control this urge to see him. I can't get him off my mind. Kaiden and my relationship was real even though we didn't say the words to each other in the month we were together. It wasn't until I was with Lincoln that he confessed his love for me. Months have passed since June, therefore I am dying to know if he still loves me. I'm also curious if I still feel the same for him. I'm pretty sure my love for him hasn't faded at all. I have butterflies just thinking about seeing him. Gosh I don't want to wait any longer!

I cash out of the machine I'm on. I quickly make my way to my room to get my jacket. My heart flutters in my chest. I don't need to see Kaiden to know I still love him. The way my body reacts when I think about him is enough to know Kaiden could very well be the man I marry.

I rush out of the hotel and start walking toward Vibe. Gaetano and Kaiden's businesses are not that far apart. It would take me longer trying to get a cab than to just walk. I think back to when I tried to see him back in August as I walked. I was so messed up when I went to Vibe and it was closed. I cared so much that he didn't see me with another man. My nerves were on edge until I left Vegas with Kirby. I hated being in Vegas and not being able to be with him.

I reach Vibe and pull on the door and step inside. The music is as loud as ever. The upper and lower dance floors are packed and so is the bar. I scan every inch looking for Kaiden. I make my way through the crowd to the bar. I don't recognize anyone working. Something doesn't feel right. I don't feel like I'm in the same place. Nothing here feels like Kaiden at all. My eyes travel over the club one more time. The sign

CHAPTER 13

that hung on the wall that said Vibe is gone. I squeeze my way back through the people and I go for the long dark hallway. The problem with that, there is no hallway anymore. A wall replaced what used to be open space. I'm confused. I don't understand.

I work my way outside and stand near the edge of the sidewalk, practically in the street. *"Whirl? What the hell?"* I say out loud. Am I lost? I hurry over to the bouncer.

"Excuse me, I think I'm lost. I'm looking for Vibe."

"You are in the right place."

"I don't think I am."

"Vibe is now Whirl." He turns away from me.

Why would the name change? Where the hell is Kaiden? I take off running back to Seven Jewels. Gaetano might know what the hell is going on. I cross my fingers that he does.

I'm out of breath from running, but that doesn't stop me from asking to see Gaetano. The desk clerk looks at me sideways. I don't have time for this shit. I need to know where Kaiden is. Finally the clerk tells me Gaetano is on the eighth floor dealing with an issue. He tells me he'll send a message to him. Fuck that! I take off for the elevators. I'll find Gaetano on my own. When I reach the eighth floor, I hurry as I walk the halls looking for any sign of which room he is in. All the doors are shut tight. I try to listen for voices, but these rooms are all sound proofed. This can't be happening to me. The one time I need him to be present, I can't find him anywhere. I tell myself to think! I need the address to Kaiden's house he grew up in. There's where Wyatt told me Kaiden's been. I've only been there once. I'd never remember how to get there. I'd go to his place here, but I have a feeling he won't be there.

"Ciara, what's going on?"

"I need to know if you know the address to Kaiden's childhood home."

He looks at me with shock written all over his face. *"I'll drive you there. It's like an hour away."*

"Do you know what happened to Vibe?"

"Let me just finish this then I'll drive you. I'll only be a minute."

A minute feels like an eternity. An hour! That's going to do wonders for my nerves. I need to take a deep breath and calm down. I'm going to be a train wreck by the time I get to him. Where is Wyatt and his helicopter now? I really wish I could snap my fingers and be with him already.

"Ready?"

"Yes!"

CHAPTER 13

Gaetano is not driving as fast as I'd like, but at least we are on our way. He told me that he heard rumors that Kaiden closed the club for renovation back in August. He reopened in September, then shortly after the name changed and he doesn't know why. I didn't express how Vibe didn't feel like Kaiden anymore. I'm sure Gaetano doesn't want to hear that anyway. It's probably difficult enough for him to be taking me to his brothers knowing that I have feelings for him. I know I asked a lot by asking him for Kaiden's childhood address. I feel extremely guilty he's driving me. This hour cannot go by fast enough.

We pull up out front of Kaiden's and I only see one light on. There's no car in the driveway. He could have parked in the garage. Although it doesn't look all that safe.

"I'll wait until I know he's here."

"You don't have to do that."

"I'm not leaving you in this neighborhood until I know he's in there."

"Thank you."

I get out and walk on shaky legs to the front porch. I don't hesitate when I knock. I check the door handle without waiting for him to answer. I am blown away when I step inside. I feel like someone punched me in the gut.

"Kaiden, are you here?"

I tiptoe around the house that used to have walls. Again, I don't feel Kaiden's presence. This place is torn apart. Every room has been gutted. Not one single wall remains. I go to what used to be a living room and see the only thing that tells me I'm in the right house. Pictures of Kaiden as a baby lay out in a photo album on the floor where a coffee table used to sit. I bend to pick it up, running my fingertips over his baby face.

"Where are you, Kaiden?"

I fall to my knees. I feel weak and sick to my stomach. Only thing that comes to mind is he didn't wait for me to come back. I can't smell his cologne lingering in the air. There's absolutely no sign he's been here other than the destruction. I feel completely empty. Empty as this house.

I don't know how I got the strength to get off my knees and walk out of his place. I sit on the front porch, praying he comes back. I cannot hold back the tears as they stream down my face like a damn just has been broken. My heart feels shattered. I feel it in my gut, Kaiden is gone! I thought he loved me? How could he do this to me?

"*Ciara, is he inside?*"

"*No. He's gone. He didn't love me enough to wait.*"

"*That doesn't make sense to me. Kaiden taking off with unsolved business isn't how he functions.*"

"*How do you know? You don't even know him.*"

"*I know enough.*"

"*That's not true. He has unfinished business with you and your father. I don't see him sticking around for him to fix that.*" I get off the porch. Now I'm angry. How the fuck could he do this to me? "*Can you take me back to the hotel please?*"

"*I can.*"

I am getting my shit and getting the hell out of Vegas and never returning. If he loved me so damn much, you don't run. I thought he was stronger than this. I thought he had more control over himself than this. A decent man would have stuck around for love.

CHAPTER FOURTEEN
CIARA

Coming back home is a complete blur. I have been in bed the past two days. I think my heart is truly shattered into a million pieces. I don't have the strength to get out of bed. All I want to do is forget Kaiden Marcellus existed. I wish I never let him have any part of me. I wish I had never met him at all. I am angry I let him into my life and he didn't have the decency to stick around like a real man should. I was ready to tell him I loved him and that time didn't change those feelings for me. No amount of tears can wash away the pain I'm feeling. I wanted him to believe in me while I worked out my feelings for the other guys.

I sit up in my bed, the realization hitting me in the face. I am such a selfish bitch. I expected Kaiden to just wait around for me to work out my feelings for the other guys? What kind of monster am I? I'm not the only person who has emotions tied up in this fucked-up mess. I seriously need fucking mental help. Who am I to ask any one of these men to wait for me? I'm nothing special. Clearly I'm not worth waiting for. I need to just let them all go. I need to tell Kirby and Malcolm to move on and forget me. They are genuine men that deserve someone who had her shit together. That someone isn't me.

I throw myself back to the mattress and cover my entire body with the comforter. I am weak. I want to take a page out of Kaiden's book and just disappear into thin air. I want to take the cowards way out. But I can't do that. I have to be an adult and not ghost someone.

I tell whoever is at the door to go away. I hear the door open anyway. I am in no mood for anyone to talk to me.

"Ciara, I know you know this, but Thanksgiving is in one week."

"Yep, I'm aware."

"Do you know if you'll have a guest this year?"

"Probably the usual."

"Just Porter?"

"Yep!"

"What's going on with you?"

"Gee, Grams, I don't know! Maybe your fucking

stupid auction has ruined my life! I fucking will never forgive you for this!"

"Watch your language with me, young lady."

"Or what? You'll kick me out? News flash, Grams, I have an apartment."

"Oh, I see how it is. You fell in love with someone and now I'm the bad guy."

"Yep! I did fall in love and now he's gone. To top it all off, I have to see Wyatt and break it off with him. I don't want to do that."

"If you don't want to do that then why do you have to break up? You two were together under my roof. I'd have to be blind if I did not see the connection between you two. Didn't the man find your father? He's damn near perfect in my book."

"Ugh!"

"Darlin, I know one of these guys hurt you. I don't know which one because you won't tell, but maybe it's for the best. I want a man for you who is going to love you and always be there for you. He needs to hold your hand, to listen to you, and love you unconditionally. I need to know somebody is going to take care of my girl when I'm not here anymore."

"I can take care of myself."

"That's not what I mean and you know it."

"Grams, it just really hurt when I went to find him

and he was gone. I was feeling so confident that he could have been the one."

"Clearly he doesn't know what he lost. You've told me before you are fond of more than one man. Maybe now you can concentrate on one of them."

"Actually, I'm thinking more along the lines of staying single."

"If that is what you truly believe is right, who am I to argue. Just try to keep an open mind when you break off the rest of your relationships."

Grams gets off my bed. *"I'll try, but it's not looking good."*

"I need you home for Thanksgiving, Ciara. Promise me you'll be here."

"I promise."

She exits my room and I cover my face again. I'm so fucking confused. She's right, I do have feelings for Kirby and Malcolm. Then there's Wyatt! I fell in love with him as well. I might have been putting all my faith into the wrong guy.

CHAPTER FIFTEEN
CIARA

I got up this afternoon and took a shower. I didn't feel much better than I did before. The hot water, the fresh smell of soap didn't do anything to make me feel alive. I literally feel like a part of me has died. I am at a loss as to how to get back to feeling whole. In my head I know Grams is right, I do have other amazing men that I had or still have feelings for. I can stay in the state I'm in or I can pull myself together somehow and move on. I'm not going to know if that's possible unless I try. By trying, I'm flying to see Wyatt. He's the last man I have to end a relationship with or build one with. Then I have to decide what I'm going to do with Malcolm and Kirby. I was serious when I told Grams I might stick to being single. It sure as hell hurts less.

"Where are you off to?"

I set my bag down by the door and open the coat

closet. *"I'm going to see Wyatt."*

"Are you sure you are ready to do that? Just this morning you were ready to stay single."

"And I may very well stay that way. I never said I was going to confess my undying love for him."

"I was hoping you would see that," she stops mid-sentence.

"Hoping what?"

"Never mind."

"Please, Grams, don't hold back now. I mean after all it wouldn't be like you to hold your tongue."

"Have a good trip, dear."

I pick up my bag, then open the door. Ugh! Damn that woman.

"I love you," I yell down the hall.

"Love you, too."

I shut the door and went after her. *"I'm sorry. I'm not purposely trying to be a bitch to you."*

"If you are hurting, you can't take it out on just anyone who walks in your path."

"I know." I sit down next to her in the sun room. *"Have you ever felt so goddamn lost that you don't even feel like yourself?"*

"A few times in my life. Want to know what happens after you find yourself again?"

"Of course."

"You become even stronger than you were before."

"How does a person become unlost?"

"You have dig down deep and pull yourself out of whatever it was that made you get lost in the first place."

"I wasn't lost being who I was before I dated these ten men."

"Are you lost because your heart is lost or because you have grown and changed from the girl who was over worked and under socialized?"

"Maybe both."

"I believe your heart will be found when you listen for its beat."

"I better go or I'm going to miss my flight."

I give Grams a hug. I hope this talk helps me before I see Wyatt.

"Ciara, I know you very well. Maybe you should take a day or two more to process what you've been through."

"Thanks. I think I've already processed the last few days, and weeks."

"But have you the last ten months?"

"I'll see you in a few days." I kiss her cheek.

CHAPTER 15

I knock on Wyatt's door and I get no answer, so I walk around to the side of the house and take the stairs. When I reach the roof top, he isn't up here either. I walk around and look out at the view. I just love it here. It's one of my favorite places I've been. I lean on the railing, looking over the scenery that goes on for miles. I watch a flock of birds that take off, chasing each other with wind beneath their wings. I wonder if being a bird is as carefree as it looks.

A noise gets my attention and I jog over to the other side of the roof. I smile. Of course he arrives home in a helicopter. I turn and run down the stairs when I see him getting out.

Wyatt unlocks his door. *"Hey,"* I say, stopping a few feet from him.

He looks to his right and his beautiful blue eyes meet my brown ones. *"Ciara!"*

I step forward, falling into his chest and wrap my arms around him. I hug him tightly. He kisses the top of my head. I begin to cry when his arms embrace me.

"That's some welcome home."

I lift my cheek off his chest. His knuckles brush along my cheek. I close my eyes.

"Sweetheart."

I open my water filled eyes. His eyes search for

what's going on.

"I'm lost, Wyatt. I don't know if I can find myself."

"You'll only be lost a short time. Eventually, everyone can find themselves." I can't talk. Words just won't form. My entire body is shaking and the tears just keep coming on stronger. *"Let's go inside. It's chilly out here."*

"I don't want you to let me go."

Wyatt reaches over one handed and opens the door. I don't know how I manage to get inside. He closes the door and then he removes my coat. I stand here unable to move once again. He takes his coat off, then he lifts me, cradling me in his arms. He takes us to the sofa and when he sits, I end up on his lap. I bury my face in the crook of his neck and shoulder. His hand brushes my hair in the back. I adjust and hold him tighter. I want him to hold me until the hurt is gone. Until there are no more tears to cry.

"You can talk to me, baby. I'm here for whatever you need."

"I just want to stay like this for now."

We stay like this for a long time. Wyatt doesn't pressure me into talking. He doesn't ask me to get off his lap or anything. He just holds me as I asked him to do. I know I can't stay like this forever, but it feels really nice just to be held by strong, stable arms. If I were to end up with him, I'd never feel unsafe. Wyatt is a protector through and though. He's also very level headed. He seems to know right from wrong. The lessons he learned from the neighbors growing up. I can't honestly say Wyatt has any faults at all. I know nobody is perfect, but he's damn close. If I were to fully commit myself to him, I think we'd have a good life together. We'd probably be a great couple until we're old and gray. Something deep inside me tells me I need to find myself again. Somewhere along the line I lost who I am. I don't know when that happened. Maybe it happened the moment I knew Kaiden was gone. It could have been when this journey of love all started. Hell, maybe I have always been lost my entire life and I'm just now recognizing it. I am unsure of so many things right now. I feel like I'm in this deep dark hole and I have no way of digging myself out. One thing I do know, I don't want to be alone. I want to share my life with someone. I think I want children at some point, as well. Curling up next to someone and having them embrace the good, bad, and ugly sure feels better than facing it alone. I just don't know who's arms I need to be in. My options are wide open at this point. A few doors have closed, but not all of them. I have to be honest with myself if I want to be honest with the remainder of the guys. Now is a good time to start. I know I'm not ready to make a decision. I can't force myself into choosing who I should be. I need to wait for the answer to come to me on its own time. I am not going to ask Wyatt, Kirby, or Malcolm to wait. There's a great possibility none of Grams men are meant to be my everything.

I sit upward and touch Wyatt's gorgeous face. His blue eyes are so damn blue! I see how he looks at me. He does care about me. He said before that he loves me. I tilt my head and rest my forehead to his.

"Thank you."

"You are welcome."

"I came here because I wanted you to know that I'm messed up. I have all these emotions pulling me in different directions. I feel lost in knowing which way to go."

"I'm sure I might be as well if I were in your shoes."

"But you're not, right?"

"No, I'm not. I know the kind of life I want for myself. I know I want a wife and maybe kids. My plan is to be happy. I built this home to share it with the right person. When I first laid my eyes on you in Millie's kitchen, I knew I wanted that somebody to be

you. The feeling that swept over me when you tried sneaking in without being noticed, I can't describe it. Love at first sight, maybe it was. The more I got to know you, the more I wanted you. I know I love you and I know that isn't going to stop."

"I can tell what you are telling me is true. In order for me to know I can love you or anyone for that matter, I need to find me again. I want no regrets."

"I understand that to a point."

"I did fall in love with you."

"Then be with me, Ciara. I will promise to make you happy every day of your life."

"I know. If I'm going to be with you, I need to make sure I love you and only you. I can't give you that right now."

"How much time are you asking for?"

"I don't know."

"Another month? A year?"

"I don't know. I'm not asking for you to wait forever."

"I don't get what you want from me. Am I your boyfriend? Am I one of many boyfriends? I can tell you right now, I shared you once and I cannot do that again."

"I'm not going to date multiple men ever again. I

need time alone to figure it out."

"It sucks when I can see the future in front of me and you can't."

I get off his lap. Why can't I see what he sees? This man is incredible. I want to take the leap of faith with him. Something is holding me back.

"I'm sorry. Please don't hate me, Wyatt."

He gets to his feet and grabs my face. *"I might be a little angry right now, but I don't hate you. I could never in a million years hate you."*

Wyatt brings me to his body and wraps his arms around me. He kisses my head. I hug him. What the hell am I doing? Am I really going to walk away from him? Will I ever come back if I do? I'm so scared I'm messing up my entire future. Why can't my head just stop playing games with me? Why am I so goddamn broken?

Wyatt's lips are on mine in a flash. I give in to his kiss. I need to put distance between us before I make more mistakes like I did with Hawk.

"I should probably go."

"Let me take you home. You don't need to be sitting in an airport right now."

I nod my head. His fingers run across my lips. Disappointment is as clear as day in his eyes. Once again I am to blame. I hurt another amazing man.

CHAPTER SIXTEEN
CIARA

I came back from Wyatt's and asked Porter to come over. I didn't want to be alone. Two mornings later, he convinced me to come to work with him. I couldn't think of a better distraction, so I went. I thought I was doing fine until he told me to go hide in the back. Grams ended up calling me to ask what kind of pie Porter likes. It's the same pie every year. I think she just wanted to check up on me. After we hung up, I started looking at material. Thanksgiving is a few days away, I thought I might as well make a new dress for the occasion. Grams is huge on getting all decked out for holidays. Even though I could care less about any holiday right this minute, it gave me something to do. I'd rather design or sew clothing than sit in a corner and sulk. I've cried enough tears for ten women. I'm trying my damndest to get out of this funk. It's hard to concentrate when all you wanted to do was cry.

A few more days passed by in a blur. All I did was make dresses. The way Porter sees it is that at least I'm doing something. I can feel myself easily falling back into the old me. The girl who is just going through the motions of a working girl. The more I worked with material the less I was thinking and the more I was ignoring my problems. In the back of my mind I know it isn't healthy. It isn't fair to guys I'm supposed to be sorting out my feelings for. I simply just don't want to think anymore. In my logical mind I know it isn't fair to them. Selfishly, I don't care much, I just want to be the old me for a while. I'm just too damaged and I am literally mentally exhausted.

I hold the dress up in front of me that I just finished making. Ugh! I don't like it. I hang it on a hanger and set it with the others. At this rate, l I'll be wearing jeans and a sweater. Grams would be so upset at me.

I turn off the lights and go out front. It feels good to be back in my store. Yet, I don't feel the same. I tell Porter we are going to close up. He looks at me like I have two heads. He reaches for my forehead and I slap his hand away.

CHAPTER 16

"Go home! I'm changing things around here."

"What does that mean?"

"Means we are changing our hours. No more working past five."

"Where is Ciara and what have you done to her?"

"I'm not sure. I'll let you know when she returns."

I turn the sign on the door to closed. I am serious about new hours. One thing I learned from Adler, decent work hours are a must for a successful relationship. Overworking is unhealthy.

We lock up and before I leave I grab all the dresses. Maybe tomorrow I'll change my mind about one of them. I say goodbye to Porter and tell him I'll see him tomorrow. I plan on doing nothing for the rest of the night besides relaxing. A nice hot bubble bath sounds good. Maybe I'll raid Grams wine cellar, too.

CHAPTER SEVENTEEN
CIARA

I didn't sleep very well last night. I was relaxed from the bubble bath, but then I got under the covers and my mind went into overdrive. I thought about Wyatt. I think he was truthful when he told me he was angry. I didn't think about it at the time, but damn he was straight forward with me. He might be the only one who expressed he was angry with me. The other guys didn't have to tell me, I could see it on their faces, but words are needed at times. I needed to hear him say he's angry. He has every right to feel that way. Every right to tell me. I don't blame him. If I were him I'd be mad at me, too. Hell, I am mad at me. That's just one of the many emotions going on inside of me. Then I thought about Kirby. He's such a respectful man. His values are family oriented. I realized I held back for a reason. I know I asked him to give me time, but I was wrong. He should be angry with me. I might have led him to believe we could be right for one another. The truth is, I don't think we are. He's easy to talk to, but when it comes to me, I still hold back. That reason alone is why he isn't right for me. When I think about Malcolm, I think we have a special bond. I can't separate whether it is friendship or relationship. In a lot of ways, it's almost like he's a brother I never had. The things we did together are things he does with his sister and mother. Besides the sex we had, everything else is what makes me think this way. It's like I have another Porter. I have really messed this dating shit up. I might not be ready for commitment because I have no clue what I am doing. Why can't I separate love and friendship?

Grams is at my door with a grin on her face. "Ciara, I need you in the family room."

"Right now?"

"Yes, you might want to throw some clothes on first, though."

"I'll be there in a minute."

"Happy Thanksgiving, dear."

"Happy Thanksgiving."

I roll my eyes when she leaves. I don't have much to be thankful for this year. I've made a train wreck of my life and hurt people in the process. I'm not proud of any of it. It really bothers me to my core. It's like if I keep saying I hurt people it will change, but that is nowhere near being true.

I put my hair up in a messy bun on top of my head. I change out of the silk nightie I was wearing and throw on leggings and a t-shirt. Before I leave my room, I slip into my slippers.

I hear voices the closer I get to the family room. One of them is Grams and I don't recognize the other. I wish she told me we had company. I would have dressed nicer.

My eyes go wide when I enter the family room. *"Ciaro!"*

"There she is!"

"What are you guys doing here? I didn't think I'd see you until after the new year."

"Someone told us we shouldn't wait to start being a family. We lost too many years already."

I go to him and hug him. *"Thank you. You have no idea what this means to me."*

"No thanks needed, you are my daughter."

Once I let go of him, I give Molena a big hug. Then I am introduced to my half-sister, Celine and her boyfriend, Brock. I hug my sister then Brock to welcome them both. I look at Grams and she smiles. This brightens my day so much.

"I hear you are having a difficult time. Want to tell me about it?"

"Maybe later. I want to hear about your trip. How long are you staying?"

"We leave on Sunday."

"Why don't I get some hot tea and a little snack for all of us. Dinner isn't for a few more hours."

"Thanks, Grams."

We all have a seat in the family room. I can't stop smiling. This has really made me so happy. I am over the moon ecstatic to have a sister.

⁂

Molena has decided to take a nap before dinner. Celine, Brock and Grams went to the city for a little shopping. I think everyone left to give my father and I time together. As much as I am enjoying their company I'd love some time with Ciaro. I don't know him well, but his face shows concern. I can bet he's worried about the dark circles under my eyes. I, on the other hand, don't want to spoil this wonderful warm feeling inside.

"Celine is thrilled to get to know you. She's always wanted a sibling."

"I am just as thrilled. She seems really nice."

"She's a good girl."

"How long has she been with Brock?"

"A couple of years."

"That's nice."

"What's troubling you, my child?"

"I had high hopes for love and it feels like a dead end road."

"If it's a dead end, turn around and find a new direction."

"You make that sound so easy."

"Sometimes going on a road that's been traveled, could lead you where you want to go."

"The mistakes that have been made, I don't care to relive them. Besides I am still on the road that needs to be finished."

"Love didn't find you with all these men your grandmother set in place?"

"It did. The problem is I can't make a solid commitment to any of them. I am overwhelmed with guilt."

"You shouldn't feel guilty about taking a chance on love."

I nod my head. I really want to change this conversation. I need a break from my ever flip flopping thoughts.

"I just want to focus my attention on you being

here. I've overthought enough and it is exhausting."

"Fair enough."

"What do you normally do on Thanksgiving?"

"When I met Molena she didn't know what Thanksgiving was. I introduced her to it."

"Really!?"

"Yep. It was wonderful. So now because I'm American we celebrate."

"That's really cool."

Ciaro and I continue to learn about one another. We spent over an hour talking before Grams, Celine and Brock came back. He went to check on Molena.

My father makes everything seem so simple. I wonder if he were in my life sooner if I'd still have relationship troubles. Maybe I would not be so afraid of commitment. I'm terrified of getting my heart broken by loving someone and then they leave me like my mother did. Where did that thought come from? I'm scared of serious commitment? Is that why I dated men like Hunter?

"Ciara, dinner is in an hour. How about you and Celine get ready together?"

"An hour? I haven't even showered yet!"

"You best get your butt in gear. Celine is in the living room with Brock."

"Okay, thanks." I go to walk around her, but stop

and kiss her cheek. *"Thank you, Grams, for inviting my father here,"* I say, giving her a hug.

"You are welcome."

※

My sister and I got ready together. She saw the dresses I made and fell in love with the beige one I made. We are the same size, so I let her have it. Me, I chose to wear an all black, silk button up dress I made. We both wear ankle, heeled boots. As I do my hair, we talk about her and Brock. I asked her how she knows he's the one, and she told me, you just know. How does everyone just know?

By the time I got my hair curled, and started applying makeup, Porter came bursting into my room. I was super excited for him to meet my new family. He's going to love them, and they will love him. Celine thinks he's funny already.

Grams sent Brock to come and get us. I put some lip gloss on and left my room. As we sit at the table in the formal dining room, my heart is happy. Grams and I have never had this many people for a Thanksgiving dinner before. Sometimes it's just her and I, other times Porter is with us. This, this feels like a real family holiday. I could get used to this.

My father is doing the honors of cutting the turkey. Then we fill our plates before we say Grace. Just when everyone digs into all the delicious food, I look at everyone sitting here. Grams and Porter are talking, Ciaro and Molena are sharing a special look, and Celine and Brock are giggling. Everything is perfect, except I feel something is missing. I pick up my wine glass and take a big sip. I'm not afraid of commitment. I did fall in love with one man above the rest. I want him to be my best friend, my lover, and the father to my children.

"Excuse me for a minute," I say getting up from the table. When I am out of the dining room, I run down the hall, up the stairs, and down another hall to my room. I get my cell off the dresser. Pulling up the contact list, I scroll to his name. Then I cross my finger as I tap the call button. Please, please answer! My heart falls to my toes when it just rings and rings. My knees feel weak when he doesn't answer.

"Where the hell are you, Kaiden Marcellus?"

He may not have answered, but I have every intention of finding him. It won't be today or even tomorrow, but I will find him. I cannot live the rest of my life without facing him. Right now, though, I have a family dinner to get through. I have so much to be thankful for, more than what I thought possible.

ABOUT THE AUTHOR

Thank you so much for taking the time to read Grandma's Silent Auction - November. Word-of-mouth is crucial for any author to succeed. If you enjoyed the book, please leave a review on Amazon. Even if it's just a sentence or two. It would make all the difference and would be very much appreciated. – OXOX Michael James

Michael's Links:

Website: http://michaeljames-author332.bravesites.com/

ALSO BY MICHAEL JAMES

If you enjoyed Grandma's Silent Auction - November, you may also like my other books:

The Way We Love series:

Pink Skies At Night

Shadows At Night

Nights Are Unlimited

Concealed By The Night

Shattered At Night

Freed At Night

Winning A Cowgirl's Heart - Trilogy:

The Rodeo King

The Best Friend

The Fate Of My Heart

Winning a Cowgirl's Heart -Complete Box Set

Construction Vs. Corporate- Trilogy:

Unbalanced

Balancing

Balanced

Secrets Within a Club

Club Comrade

Revenge

Saving Club Conrad

Masquerade Saga

His Pearls

His Secrets

His Prison

His Games

His Moves

All His

Crime in Landkaster series

The Mirror

Times Like These

Lonely Road of Faith

Grandma's Silent Auction series

January

February

March

April

May

June

July

August

September

October

Lost Love Letter

I'll be Waiting

Before I Do

Standalone:

Toying With October

Pieces Of Me

A Christmas For Eve

Dom Diaries: Tangled Up In You

Christmas Scavenger Hunt

Blue Christmas

Stealing the Christmas Spotlight

Co-written with Jodi Fahey

Last Sheet

Co-written with Daniel Grayson

Inside the Storm

Manufactured by Amazon.ca
Bolton, ON

44916154R00074